REFRIGERATOR CHURCH

Paul Nelson

TP

TAILWINDS PRESS

Tailwinds Press
P.O. Box 2283, Radio City Station
New York, NY 10101-2283
www.tailwindspress.com

Published in the United States of America
ISBN: 978-0-9975742-6-5
1st ed. 2019

CONTENTS

REFRIGERATOR CHURCH

DOG WATCH

Sam drifted in the clanging of bells. His stomach wallowed. He tried to lift his head from the bunk.

Fire bell...from the town hall. Darlene's body falling and rising on the swell just off the end of the landing... her hands caught in the white, frozen folds at her throat, black dress a fan, lacy with spring salt-ice. Heart-shaped face the color of kerosene. Clang. Clang.

Ship's bell. End of first dog watch. Drifting off again.

Above her, the Crawford boys swaying in the skiff and hanging onto the lobster warp clove-hitched to her ankle above the high-topped shoe, as if she were a fish too large to haul. Faces like onions. Ellie's face peeking, half-smothered in Rosa's coat. Other faces from town. Dr. Harmon, grim, hare-lipped, waving his white hand, mumbling to beach her. Men staring at their boots. Ellie, green-gray as the top side of a halibut, her eyes pinched, face fear-wrenched. The fire bell blanging above the town as if it weren't too late. In the bow of the skiff, pronged seven-foot spears, three pails of squirming, wounded eels.

Six bells. Sam finally counted . . . six, second dog-watch. Dawn.

He swung his legs over the edge of the bunk, felt his feet land on the deck. Sat up slowly. Ellie would be very mad at his drinking. But she was so far away. Way away from the picture that had started to rise with his nausea at the end of the old one. He stood. His pictures were bad.

Above decks, in the light rising, in working whites, Sam inhaled deeply; the salt air bunged his lungs, made him cough, then clear. He sought his bearings by looking across the silver-nitrate bay at the brightening horizon. Yachts, tenders, skiffs and day-sailors, trawlers and lobster boats crowded the view. Dark shapes like coffins. He wanted them gone. He wanted to be gone, weigh anchor and raise sail, be out on the clean.

Lowering the bosun's chair over the rail, he slowly tied it off, clove then half-hitch, raised one leg and then the other over, and, rolling to face the hull, shinnied down, knot to knot, to the yoke. He writhed and worked his legs and ass into the canvas seat. Knees to the hull, he hung there, mastering his gut.

He leaned in. Forehead against the black, cool, salt-filmed ship. As he did in winter, forehead against the jersey's warm loin, his fingers aching with cold, with splitting wood, foolish on the hot teats. He pushed away to flex and stretch his legs, tried to crack his knuckles through the crystal morning ache tolling in his fingers. Pettigrew leaned down over the rail, his shaved face shining, shouting "Yo!" as his arms lowered the first bucket. Sam put his hand into the cold, fresh water and fished for the slimy skin. The numbing was good. He dropped the chamois back into the bucket, hung in the canvas sling, sorting pictures.

Black rows of beets and potatoes, red dirt and white flannel rags flapping from stakes to keep away the jays and ravens. Ellie's rosebush, wild pink on the trellis by the kitchen door. Sour smelling peonies along the picket fence. The two gray plum trees, their longest branches broken down by coons that hung like ditty bags to reach the fruit. Light bulbs in the downstairs rooms, taking away the warm shadows, the warm smell of kerosene. Ellie's idea.

He fished again for the chamois, wrung it out and started to wipe away the salt-film from the black, japanned hull. His shoulder circled in grit. He wiped harder, wider, waking. Ellie, and gray Baby Eva in six inches of gray water in the galvanized tub on the cow-chewed lawn, beating her gray doll into the suds. More and more coming clear as he tried to keep with his visions, home, far away. Suddenly his face in the lacquer, wet leather swimming on a skull. His stomach surged. Ants scurried under his eyelids on the black, slicey leaves of Ellie's peonies. He looked away, along the water-line. Teetering punts hauling themselves along the hull like wounded ants, crew wiping and wiping, bantering before breakfast. He wanted coffee, thick and hot and black. The bumping of the punts against the hull made him hear again the one hard bump the night before.

"Son of a bitch," the Steward had said, lantern waving by his ear as he leaned out, looking down from the eyes at the bow where the bump had come. The forward watch staggered, just back from town, some too drunk to lay down yet, afraid of swimming in their bunks. In the yellow light of the lamp, helped by the scant moon rising over the spruce head, an ivory girl on her stomach, one leg pulled up, arms wide, palms flat on the gray planks of one of the rafts that kids swim and dive from all summer. Dead, Sam thought, running, clambering down the midships ladder, missing rungs, almost falling from the tipsy punt as they tried to keep their balance and pull themselves forward along the hull, the Steward barking for the Mate.

Rolling her over. Bits of red and yellow caught in the oily, boozy bile slicking her chin, tits and stomach, fouling her pale bush. Sam's stomach heaved again, nothing coming up. He kept on wiping, as if to wipe through his face, through the picture. He remembered his hand behind her head, in the sticky, sandy tangle. She'd moaned. The hair cold.

He stopped wiping, whistled for Pettigrew, sent the

bucket up to be refilled. He waited, knees and forehead against the hull. The Captain and Mate had loomed up along the rail in robes and slippers, white ankles, ordering them to wrap her easy in the blanket they tossed down. More crew coming up, sleepy in skivvies, pants with suspenders over their bare shoulders, white feet at eye-level. The Mate's torch hit her, moved off. Sam remembered lifting her as the Steward pulled the blanket under her arms and around, covering the messed body. He remembered her dead, helpless weight over his shoulder, up the few rungs of the jigging ladder, his legs struggling, many hands taking her from him. The Mate, always cheery, saying, "OK. Boys. Break it up now."

Then standing with the Steward in the passageway, crowding the narrow door to Stateroom #2, the Captain wiping her down with a warm towel. Dabbing her face, tits and belly, diving between her thighs. Then topside, running to the stern, the moon snaking up the clean.

A new bucket swayed down. The sun began to heat his shoulders. He wrung fresh water over his head. Alive, he thought . . . ivory. He flushed . . . tits not big, just solid. Thighs damp, gold in the kerosene lamp's glow. He hoped the Captain hadn't seen him looking. "You're all right, Missy . . . we'll watch you," the Captain had said, tucking the blanket under her chin.

Ivory face in moonlight. Then Darlene. Black taffeta and lace. Ellie gray in the chairless parlor crowded with tall red and white gladiolas, bending, kissing her sister's pumiced cheek. Rosa ministering, making women and children look. The girl bubbling at the Captain, "Don't," then, "Thank you very much," sagging back.

Sam wiped and wiped to make the *Ramala* shine.

Toward midmorning, Sam was splicing line in the narrow shade of the main mast when they brought her up on deck. They'd let her dress in one of the Owner's whore's dresses, blue velvet with sewn pearl front. She was barefoot, her peach face swollen like Baby Eva's after sleeping hard, or crying. Her eyes squinted in the morning light and her mouth was quivery. But her strawberry hair was all brushed out, smooth and easy. He stared at her feet. She was no townie. Her back was straight, chin tucked. The Steward, in starched whites for the occasion, padded up to her with the heavy silver tray, china cups and silver coffee pot. He put the tray down on the after hatch and poured for the girl. The Captain and Mate poured for themselves. They talked, but Sam couldn't hear. Townies have dingy hair, he thought. He thought of "Venus on the half-shell," what Miss Aquadine called the picture in the fat book of famous pictures. The girls giggled and the Crawfords, all in the same class, but different ages, stifled. Darlene had sneezed on laughter.

Putting her cup down, she walked to the rail. Light caught on her feet, ankles, forearms, face and hair as she slowly stepped down, glowing, rung to rung, then moved under the canopy of the Owner's launch. Sam went to the rail. Pettigrew swung the launch toward shore and Sam waved once, his wrist against his chest, at the back of her head, burning in shade. He wanted desperately to go fix something, stack wood, run errands, wipe the hull.

That afternoon, Sam racked a game of nine-ball and took the first swig of cold ale to settle his stomach. He studied each shot, ball to ball, then caromed the nine off the six into the side pocket. The Steward shrugged, started to rack them up again, but Sam gave up the table and went back to the bar. The Steward, hauling at his trousers, offered Sam a whiskey. "Save your life," he said. Sam wanted to stay clear. The ale cooled him. The Steward sucked his teeth and said, "I wonder what the little bitch is up to now? Probl'y a flock of maids sousing her in bubble bath. Christ she stunk!" Sam winced, sprinkled salt in his ale, watched the head come up. All afternoon he'd been incanting, "The Girl on the Float," as if she'd been a painting. It sounded right, like the lady's name he couldn't remember, the one in the red velvet dress, red-gold hair shining, that Miss Aquadine read to them about, who lived in a tower over a river, just waiting. Sam was happy that she was up there. Happy with the story. She wasn't a big, dead mermaid.

Glasses off, he thought, Ellie looks as if she doesn't know what to do. That's best, sometimes, but she wears them all day long, except to wipe them, until she goes to bed, just before she blows out the lamp. Wire the upstairs too, this winter. Never lets me see, except by mistake, like when she's in the tub with the door a little open . . . the two of them, gray, playing and laughing in the gray water. Kisses with her lips stiff, turns her head when I try my tongue. The gurgling, wounded sound when I'm pumping away. Come right away then. Gets up in the dark and goes into the bathroom and shuts the door. Never lets me see her face when she makes that sound. Always in the dark. Her pee sizzling behind the door.

The Steward was talking. As if he'd been listening, Sam looked at his flat, Algonquin face. Others, with crew from other yachts, came in. The room grew smoky and loud. The Steward ordered a steak sandwich. A big fellow with a fighter's bud nose, wearing a stained, tan turtleneck and battered fedora with his deck sneakers still on, said, " . . . on a raft." Sam tuned in. "Yah, if we'd a' done it they'd lynch us like niggahs, but we ain't from Yay-uhl." Sam's stomach jumped. His face grew hot. He made fists. The big one went on, "Like to show the little missy what a man is, not them weenies that nevah worked a day . . . damn sheep in them white sweatahs."

Sam fought not to get up, walk over and marlin-spike him in the belly. He moved back to the last stool, near the screen door. The voices drifted with the smoke through the screen. He was afraid he'd hear her name . . . Kimberly or Pamela. He thought how lobster boats and draggers have names like JANE-ANN, or DARLENE.

He got up and walked out the back, past the barrels and crates into the harbor air, fishy and soft. He walked down the pier. Boys were hand-lining for flounder under the floodlight that had just been turned on. A face-sized fish flopped on the creosoted planks. He untied the skiff and rowed hard but smoothly. A gray moon was just up, almost full, gaping at rags of sunset behind him. Way off among the hulls, under the pocked face, bits of clean line implied the horizon.

In the morning, Sam was clear. No dreams. He wiped and wiped with bigger and bigger elliptical sweeps. He rinsed and wrung out the chamois. He ordered buckets. Head at deck level, he saw over the scuppers the party come out on deck, all in white but the Brigadier. They'd come aboard during the night for a cruise to Block Island. Pettigrew was complaining again about all the ladies' luggage for one lousy weekend. The Owner draped his thick white sweater over his shoulders against the morning cool. Sam thought the bright blue Y was fine. The Brigadier's wife had on a floppy white hat, white blouse and skirt with many fine, pressed pleats, and white shoes with the damned black heels that marked the holy-stoned teak deck. The whore was tan. Sam saw her powerful ass and thigh muscles through her linen slacks. She was smoking, a long black holder under her long nose. Her forearms were tanned purple, crowded with gold bangles.

The Brigadier's wife was pasty, a real boozer. Loud. Sam watched the Captain in his black uniform suit walk aft, passing just above his head. The Brigadier leaned on the stern rail by the flag, swirling a water glass of scotch. The Steward would be coming along with their tray of coffee and Portuguese sweet-rolls. Sam climbed up and over the rail and headed for the galley.

A few minutes later, the Brigadier struggled down through the hatch into the galley, as he usually did in the morning. He had the annual bottle of Green River whiskey by the neck and passed it to the Steward with a nod. The Steward took it quickly, stored it in the locker behind the tins of baking powder, cream of tartar, sugar, salt and La Touraine coffee. The Brigadier's tan uniform shirt was open at the throat, the tan gabardine slacks razor creased. His tan shoes were spit-shined. Even his pate was tan and shining. Sitting casually among them, swigging his drink, he narrowed his eyes and said, "Well, boys, I hear you had a visitor last night, a lady caller." He looked around. No smiles. "I hear she got away with Miss Goldman's dress!" He laughed. No one said anything; the men shifted in their chairs, or looked into their coffee mugs. Sam looked down at his deck sneakers. The Brigadier took a swig, said, "Well, anyway . . . it was good to beat out Old Corny last spring! Better than the damned race! Bet he fired his crew for that one." "No," said the Steward, who was making more coffee in the big, enameled pot, "just the cook." Everyone laughed.

Sam remembered the two-hundred-foot steam yacht hoving into the broads of the river, bearing right for the *Ramala*, already anchored on Old Corny's customary marks. As the steamer came dead in the water not a hundred yards away, there was a message from the New York Yacht Club Commodore, requesting the *Ramala* to please give way. But the Owner raised the white pennant with the blue Y up the flag halyard, under pennants for Owner Aboard, New York Yacht Club, and Old Glory. Brown bottles of beer were opened for the crew, from his own brewery in Pawtucket. Through the binoculars, Sam could see Old Corny's crew scurrying. But no old man in a deck chair, slouch hat on and all wrapped in blankets— the way he looked in last Sunday's *New Haven Register* that retold last year's Eli win.

The Brigadier swallowed a bite of biscuit with butter and sugar and said, "You know Al bets against his own school?" Sam knew the Brigadier didn't care about what he said, being a West Pointer. Sam liked the low, thin sculls with the boys pulling like hell upriver. It didn't make much sense, but it got to him anyway, all the cheering and boathorns.

The Brigadier took another bite and mumbled, "Steward, you make the best goddamned biscuits in the world ... I ought to know ... Eaten 'em everywhere, and eaten every nigger food from A-rab sheep-eyes to Malay lizard."

He laughed. The Steward put down the pan and said, "Got any lizard?" They all laughed and Pettigrew said, "Maybe that would improve things around here," waving his hand at the galley. The Steward said he'd ask at S.S. Pierce.

Sam thought, the Brigadier is OK. Complaining to the Owner about the ladies wasting water washing their hair, bathing, flushing every time. Jokes about them all wearing black to match the hull, so the crew won't have to wipe down every surface they decide to put their asses down on. But white is best. Damn coal smoke and cinders, every port. And damn the hanging in a sling, wiping salt. And damn the Owner letting the party play with the helm, taking her off point, sails flapping, wind on the back side. Haul the jibs so tight there isn't a twitter. Women should stay below . . . except downwind. Then it don't really matter, deck flat and easy.

The Brigadier stood up, his glass empty. "The Mrs. sends her best, boys, says you're all cute as bugs." They raised their mugs to him as he vanished up through the hatch. The Steward said, "She's got a foul mouth."

The noon watch finished mess, pans clattering into the sink. Church, the cabin boy, handed a note to the Steward, who gave Sam the high sign. Sam knew they were going to the chandlery on Water Street. It wasn't his shore-watch, but the Mate had assigned him.

He went to his cubby in the fo'c'sle and changed to

clean whites. He carried his shoes with the black rubber heels up on deck and changed from his sneakers at the rail. He climbed down into the launch, went to the red, gleaming Perkins engine and cranked the fly-wheel. It started with a clatter, smoothed out as he advanced spark. The exhaust gargled aft. Sam looked at the cushion where she'd sat in the shade under the canopy, now rolled down and off the frames. The Captain was already in the bow, smoking his pipe. He'd changed to whites. The gold buttons and braid gleamed. The Steward cast off the last line and Sam backed the launch off a little, then smoothly shifted forward and, pushing the tiller way over, swung the bow toward the town landing. It was hot, the air dead. Sticky. Sam thought, peonies won't bloom without ants all over them. Ellie doesn't know why that's so.

He looked back. Even at anchor the *Ramala* was low and racy. Sun glinted off the cocktail shaker and the coffee urn where the Owner and the whore sat in deck chairs aft. The flags were all drooped. Sam steered dreamily in and around the moored skiffs, buoys and day-sailors and spotted the gray raft, its fifty-gallon drums half-wallowing on a little stretch of sand. He thought of Dr. Harmon looking up from Darlene's frozen face: "I'd say she's been in the water about a week." Rosa already saying again how she'd thought she'd run away with one of the loggers, her money from the sardine factory all gone from where she hid it. Ellie wide-eyed. Never mentions her sister at all.

Rosa took it. She saw.

Then Sam remembered Ellie at fifteen backing down the ladder into the hot engine room of the old sardiner, the *Willoby*. Cake on her blue mouth, she blushed when she turned around and saw him in his shorts. She sneezed, coughed on the crumbs, coughed and coughed. He grabbed her to stop the coughing, whacked her on the back. Ellie cleared, turned and tried to wrestle away, but not hard. Then they were on his pallet, twisting. He fumbled down her bloomers. She cried, wild, the bloomers hanging from one foot, shoe still on. Then she was quiet. Him talking without thinking, anything to reassure her, how they would live. Maybe with Rosa, she said, the empty room. Not the *Willoby*. He'd looked around at his home and job in one. Walking through town that afternoon, toward Rosa's. People in their windows, on their porches hanging wash, knew that that was that. Girls to marry off. The oldest drowned. "Well along," Dr. Harmon had said. Ellie saying Rosa made the cake just for him. Baby Eva.

Sam shook his head, disengaged the clutch and let the launch slide around and lightly bump the landing. The Steward tied up as Sam cut the engine. A tiny breeze came up, frittering the water, making flags and pennants restless. The midday shift was coming, southwest. The bay would begin to flash. Day-sailors would show up. The Captain knocked out his pipe on the gunwale and stepped onto the pier. He was tall. Sam thought of how Miss Aquadine always said, "All's right with Heaven and God's in His World."

A big, big car hove down toward the head of the pier. A Rolls, alright, thought Sam. The Steward snatched his sleeve. Shining, longer than the launch, it geared down with a heavy clash and whine, sighed to a stop. The black-green paint shone almost as much as the mountings, trunk straps, blinding grill and radiator, all German nickel silver. The Captain strode up the pier.

Sam and the Steward followed. The Chauffeur opened the rear door as if it were a gate. His cap visor and leather leggings shone. Out stepped a tall old gentleman in a gray morning coat, black top-hat, soft gray pinstriped pants, gray spats and gleaming black shoes. He stepped to the head of the pier and waited, leaning on a silver-headed cane. Sam felt short of breath.

The Captain tipped his cap. "Sir," said the old man, "I am made to understand that you were of some service to my granddaughter the other evening." The Captain said, "Yes Sir, our pleasure," and quickly looked away. "Well, Sir," said the grandfather, "it has been no pleasure for us I assure you, but I wish to express our gratitude. I have spoken with your Owner by telephone and know that you and your crew will wish to be discreet with the details." "Of course," said the Captain. Sam was looking at the Rolls, the tasseled curtains in the dark windows, the little nickel silver nymph flying along on the radiator cap.

The old man pulled off one gray glove and shook hands with the Captain, who said, "Well, Sir, I'd like to say that it was these men here as found her." The old man didn't look their way. Sam stared at his big, gray face with the pocked nose under the bristly eyebrows. "They speak well of you, Captain. My compliments to your Owner." He nodded to the Chauffeur, turned and ducked into the dark back of the Rolls. The Chauffeur shut the door with a thunk and hung back, putting his gloved hand out to the Steward. He winked at Sam as he got behind the wheel.

The Rolls growled away uphill into town. The Steward looked into his palm, turned to Sam and said, "We'll split this," and snorted. The Captain looked, turned his head aside and spat on the paving. Sam was thinking about how dark it was in the back of the car, how she might have been in there. He thought of the silver-headed cane, shining in the dark. "It's him, alright," he said, "yacht as big as Old Corny's, only sail." The Steward pulled his sleeve.

That night, Sam lay awake on his bunk. Near sleep, he remembered the day under the barn this spring, in the gloom, his back flat and freezing on the dirt as he tried to slam a hardwood wedge between the top of a post and a sagging joist, the frost having heaved and let go. How he'd dropped the sledge, his head heavy as keel lead, his arms and legs like piled anchor chain. How strange and good it felt, the cold moving into his neck, the back of his head. Then Ellie, on one knee, head cocked sideways, spectacles glinting: "What in the world just lying there! Get up! You'll freeze! Soup's ready. Come in! I've been calling and calling."

ROYALTY

Just as I wind my rattling '73 Volvo sedan up the slope by Betty's house on the early morning's light snow, BANG! . . . lightning whacks the black transformer can, hanging on the pole opposite her house. The can explodes. I mean EXPLODES! I think shrapnel. Slowing and skidding in fear, I catch in a millisecond the crisp blue streak shoot across the wire that enters her old Cape. Smoke at the wall. Dazzled, I pull into her yard, scattering hysterical ducks and calling out the big truculent gander that guards the yard. She calls him Bothwell. I dodge out of the car, skirting the tall bird as it spreads its wings. Last year Bothwell battered the push-nose of a summer person's affectionate boxer dog that strayed from the main road, reddened one of its brown bug eyes, sent it off where it belonged. One time, he grabbed the bit of loose fabric below my butt as I scooted away. I try to like this bird. After all, I'm a guy. I have two chainsaws. But it is beyond me to understand Bothwell's will to protect this particular property, and a bevy of mallards. No legacy of goslings here. I wonder if he experiences anything like yearning when a jazzy vee of Canadas migrates south or north overhead. He seems so dedicated and pissed and strict. Captive as Bothwell in Malmo. Maybe bonded to Betty, who feeds him almost anything. As she did her dead husband, a sickly person who at least kept the place neat. Maybe Bothwell killed him. Opening the kitchen door, wisps of acrid smoke sneak out by me. "You theah?" I mimic the lingo. Betty croaks, "Course I'm heah." Fumes catch in my throat. "You OK?" "Yah." She is sitting back as usual in the faded pink chenille bathrobe she wears 24/7, in her bony wooden chair backed by a sepia bed pillow, the kitchen table strewn with pill bottles, matchbooks, her Camels, the sour ochre coffee cup. And scattered books. One of which is the fat Lacey Baldwin-Smith biography of Henry VIII that I loaned her two years ago but which she cannot give back. I don't cherish it anymore; it is hideously stained with coffee and nicotine and would smell like the kitchen . . . cat piss from the sandbox behind the kerosene heater. And now this bitter, fatal, chemical smell. But there she is, her rolled, mottled ankles vanishing in low, black canvas sneakers with no laces. Her bloated face, settled around her neck like a Renaissance "millstone" collar, puffs and blows an added amount of smoke into the low-ceilinged room. I'm no smoker, feel choked and claustrophobic. Betty, if someone touts their heritage, like the DAR "person" who came just once to interview her, would say, rearing back, "I . . . am a . . . di-rect descendant of . . . Mary, Queen of Scots!" Which also makes her the authority on everyone since Henry VIII, including FDR, Ike, and Clinton, who had, as she affirms, "issues" with their wives. She hates any mention of James VI. Says he was a "fruit" who hated his mother. The lane she was born on is called Penshawe Way. Betty Penshawe. Scottish, ancestors down from New Brunswick in the late 1600s to seek fresh trapping ground as the French receded west and north from what is now Downeast Maine. "Lookit that damn phone," she belches. The melted phone, fuming, a free-form rat, is now an artifact fused to its wall-mount cradle where the bolt of lightning insinuated itself upon Betty's sovereignty. A fixed thing, with a burnt-off strand of wire for a tail. A legend. She will never, ever have it removed. "Bothwell's peckah," she will come to call it. "Call the company when you get home, OK? I want one of them new phones I can walk around with." She means she'll keep it on the table, getting fungal. Betty doesn't "walk around." "OK," I answer, and turn to leave. At my back she says, "I'll have eggs on Saturday." Yeah, frozen. Last fall I was baking with duck eggs laid in nests around the little "pond," dammed up by her husband's husbandry from a narrow brook that trickles through the small, now overgrown field behind the house. "Half a dozen," I say. "I'll call first."

"No bothah," she says. They are big eggs. She has maybe half a dozen mallard hens tottering around the yard, looking for stale bread crumbs. One limping drake manages this harem and stays out of Bothwell's way, except that once. Betty won't use them (not that she bakes anymore either) because she's seen the ducks eat slugs. It is seldom she has eggs now, to find them in the deep, muddy grass an effort for her bulk, and I am not charmed anymore by dancing with the gander, and failing, lately, in empathy for my own species, would not have turned into her yard but for the BANG and that gorgeous, thin blue race of lightning running down her line.

REFRIGERATOR CHURCH

Winifred has the fading Polaroid on the wall of his welding shop beneath his trophy, an anodized Olympic runner breaking an imaginary tape, FIRST PLACE, MAINE STATE MEET, 440 YDS, 1929. The sheltie, a blurred orange dervish. The seal, oil-black, set on its hind flippers like a lamp... Anubis, without the jackal ears. A lady who saw the seal cross Route 1 into the shop yard pulled in, leaned out of her car window and snapped the picture. The sheltie ricocheted, it seemed, off air in front of the seal, apparently cornered by the elm tree.

Albee, full belly to the thick bench, tinkering, seething a done-me-wrong song between his teeth, comes out of the Quonset first, hearing the barks, the one crazed, automatic rifle fire, the other, occasional, containing the casual collision of rocks in a sea cave. He "psssts" the dog back up the duck walk to the Dorseys' porch and squats like a Russian power lifter, lights up a cigarette and looks into the seal's face.

"Don't seem sick, Win, not like that fuckin' thing." His round face, color of a basketball, in perpetual straight-lipped grin. He jerks his thumb at the Dorseys' porch where the Mrs. looms, roseate, behind glass. Winifred, coming along behind, lifts off his welding helmet and tucks it under his arm like a football player. "Hunh," he grunts, his lower lip pushing almost to the tip of his bubbled, henna nose. He doesn't wear his teeth when working. "Mebbe mental, though."

Lincoln stoops under the door jamb and hobbles out on his club foot with its short boot in eccentric orientation to his other leg, twisted by polio. He towers over the seal, looks closely and then points to an eight-inch welt like a strip of gum rubber plastered on its lower back. "Prop scar . . . allus dicin' around under the keel." Albee, still squatting, asks, "Wonder what got it up from the river? Must be four hundred yards . . . two fences I know of, and the beef critters." Winifred shrugs, "Tired of seals." Lincoln lifts to his wiry six feet, eight inches and says, "Ain't old. No young fool either." He looks to Winifred: "What you gonna do?"

Winifred sets his helmet on top of the vending machine outside by the door and goes around to the side of the shop obliquely facing the Dorseys' lime-colored bungalow, set back beneath maples on a little knoll. He climbs up on the bed of his truck and unties the line securing the top of a blue, sixty-gallon plastic drum with MARA-

SCHINO CHERRIES stenciled in white on the side. The painful smell of decrepit herring and lobster bait wafts up and into the breeze. He brings a scoopful and shakes a small pile out in front of the seal. The seal hauls itself near, stretches, sniffs.

Mrs. Dorsey cranks down her louvers, leans out the door. "You men, you men," she yells, "I can smell that in here!" The three men look at each other, shrug and continue watching the seal as it backs off from the sour fish and hunches over the sill and onto the cool concrete floor, then under the bench along the rear wall near the red argon welder, the ON and other lights flashing like an ambulance. "Shoulda guessed, fussy . . . only fresh," Winifred says. "Seen 'em, though, haulin' traps—grab even mushy bait a lobster wouldn't take." He returns to his truck and ties the cover back over the barrel while Lincoln takes the scoopful inside and waves it under the seal's polished, aloof nose. "Prob'ly full," he says. The seal is looking off into the distance of the Quonset, light coming in through tall, dormered windows cut in the bowed walls. Winifred comes in, goes to the yellow loader he's been working on, hauls on his helmet, picks out a brazing rod, adjusts the welding machine's juice, lowers the visor and gets down on his back on the creeper, hauls himself under the bucket. The seal watches, charmed by the sparks. Albee and Lincoln spin out of the yard and turn right toward town, clam rollers and forks jumping on the bed when the pickup bops up onto the asphalt.

Done for the day, Winifred stands up, his face magenta from lying down, head back, legs sticking out, torso swiveling around on the creeper that scritches on the floor. He rubs the back of his neck, riven like a walrus', to ease the spasms of nerves pinched years ago. He lights up a Camel. His duty-green shirt and pants are peppered with spark holes. Longjohns show through like gray skin. His hands are speckled with carbon burns and his nails look like mussel shells. He makes some notes on the back of a matchbook cover with a stub of pencil, puts his cigarette down on the edge of the charred bench and draws a chalk line on a steel plate to remember where to start in the morning. He shuts down the reciprocating, belt-driven hacksaw that has been shifting sleepily through a thick steel bar most of the afternoon. The seal is already at the doorsill. Winifred baits it up a plank into the back of his stake-body truck with a Reese's Peanut Butter Cup. He is pretty sure the seal has been a tourist attraction somewhere up the coast. He locks the shop and drives through town, the seal bouncing along and looking around between the stakes until they reach Winifred's teal-colored bungalow on Water Street, paralleling the tidal river. Nobody notices the seal's arrival in the neighborhood.

Albee and Lincoln are already parked in front, half in the street because stoves and refrigerators, washers and dryers, waiting for pickup and bills to be paid, deck the little yard in front except for the short driveway Winifred uses to back up to the porch. The names of citizens are printed in magic marker on the top of each machine: Crockett, Johnson, Olsen, Kurtz, Bagley. Arctic walls surround the building and a ziggurat rises in the back lot, trussed by a six-foot chain link fence. Waiting Frigidaires, Gibsons, Kenmores and Coldspots bulge the mesh here and there, the biggest bulge eastward at the flesh-tone, newly cedar-shingled restaurant/pub next door, its hanging sign out front depicting in gold bas-relief a salmon leaping. On the treated wood porch a chalkboard reads: Quiche, Moule, Spritzers. The owner, a pretty lady "from away," has already complained about the "junk-yard" next door. Winifred smiled, smoothed back his dirt thick hair and asked, "Why don't you just do your dishes over here, use a freezer or two, I'll hook you up good." He watched her walk away, teetering on her wedgies. "Nice double-wide she's got," he told the boys at the Lilac.

The three men squeeze down the center hallway of the bungalow, past the twine-tied bundles of magazines and newspapers, past hooks carrying a heavy mackinaw, a pea-jacket, and a black rubber slicker with yellow bands and stripes. They shoo the seal on ahead of them through the kitchen and out the back door, down the stoop and into the small open area of dirt in the back lot, all closed in by the fortress of machines inside the fence. Winifred slides an old dog collar, already cabled to the leg of an antique Estate El-O-Range, on the seal. The seal looks up at him and pulls itself to shade in a channel between upright freezers. Winifred turns the hose on to trickle in a battered turkey pan. "Whadd'ya say to this," says Lincoln and puts down a fresh mackerel from the A&P within the seal's reach. The seal grabs it with its white teeth, tosses it once to start it head first, and swallows. Albee puts his finger in his ear and digs, says, "Ya know, I'll drop a trawl goin' out and back tomorrow, see if I hit a run. Mebbe tinkers is in. We can freeze 'em. Bet it will eat thawed."

They go back through the house to sit on the front porch. When they look back later, between beers, the seal has clambered up some stairs of stacked wooden blueberry boxes onto a chest freezer and is basking. Two neighborhood cats, having smelled fish, sit on an avocado refrigerator by the fence and watch the new sort of dog. "Got an idea," says Winifred.

He and Albee wrestle a big, gray, speckled dryer with GOOCH written in magic marker on its side, walking the machine off the porch where it smiles down, level with the truck's tailgate. Lincoln clumps around, pulling the machine onto the bed. They tie the dryer in, next to the blue bait barrel, then all sit down again on the maroon car seats banked against the front wall of the house. Winifred sips ale through the few rust-colored hairs sprouting from his nostrils. His thick eyebrows chevron down as he squints against the sunset, flashing orange on the river slicks. "After suppah, I'm gonna take 'er for a swim." Albee nods, pulls a pint of Kessler from his coat and passes it. Lincoln takes a mouthful and swallows, his red-rimmed eyes watering. He chokes, "Interestin' day."

Friday. The seal has clambered backwards up the hatch of the front load door of the big gray, industrial dryer, the dryer lying on its side so the hatch makes a ramp. The dryer stands next to the vending machine in partial shade outside the welding shop. The seal has its collar on, leashed to a "C" hook Winifred has screwed into the door jamb. Shelley is ecstatic, pirouetting, barking into the dryer's cave. "God damn roaster," mutters Winifred, lifting his helmet, and the three men go out to see just as the seal emerges, waddles down the ramp, lifts itself on its tail and starts swinging its head and swiveling in the dirt to face the sheltie. The dog lunges in, teeth bared; the seal strikes like a snake, nabs the little dog by the throat and shakes it, tosses it three feet in the air to the base of the elm tree where it lies quivering. Mrs. Dorsey is barging down the duckwalk, her hair up in green neon curlers. Her face transmogrifies awe. She stops dead when the seal makes its move, then stumbles on, howling, "Jesus . . . sweet, merciful Jesus!" She lifts the dog, limp in her flaccid arms, and screams, "Beasts! Beasts!" Glaring, she struggles up the walk, the dog's head flopping over the crutch of her elbow. Her entire body quaking, she sets the little corpse down on the couch on her glassed-in porch. She is blubbering and moaning and uttering cries. White spittle foams in the corners of her grief-clowned mouth. She drops to her knees. "Jesus, Jesus," she wails. The corpse releases its urine into the brown and orange afghan.

Mrs. Dorsey stares at the dog and then steps backwards to the phone on its wall-mount by the door into the kitchen. She dials the Reverend Dorsey, who is painting chairs for the Sunday school at THE NEW FACES OF THE NAZARENE church, a brand new brick building just off Route 1 beyond the A&P. She yells, "Murder! They've murdered Shelley." And slams down the receiver, then lifts it up again, calls Gil Amery at Troop J.

By noon, Winifred's shop yard has a collection of people: three tourists with cameras, two kids swizzling around on brightly tasseled bikes, thinking about how close they can come to the entrance to the dryer where the seal has retreated, two gaffers taking things in with vacant humor, and Ned Fenetry, the local banker back from lunch. Doc Perry, who raises Scotties and is the only vet around who will leave his office for visits, has driven down from Pembroke. The clam warden from Sea and Shore Patrol scooches, reaches in and strokes the seal's underchin; she is wearing a pretty, light green summer shift and her hay-colored hair is combed down, shining on her day off. She protests, "Oh, not yet . . ." when Winifred baits the seal from the dryer and back inside the shop and under the bench. "Too young for all this," he says, smiling at her. He is wearing his teeth. Lincoln bumps in, jams on his brakes, gets out and hobbles toward the group with a big bag of hamburgers. "I saw the whole thing," he says, "That seal was calm as could be, took as much as it could stand." Winifred shakes his head, "Means business, 'at's all."

Reverend Dorsey, in a beige, three-piece suit with bell-bottom trousers and white high-top shoes with zippers down the insides of the ankles, bends here and there, picking up wrappers and straws and flip-tops, muttering, "It's a tragedy, a tragedy," his face angelic. Doc Perry puts his liver-spotted hand on Mrs. Dorsey's heaving shoulder and says he knows how she feels, having lost dogs in many ways all his life. Puffed and blowing, inconsolable, unappeasable, she croaks again and again: "Filthy," "Rabid," "It will kill a child," "It smells," and "It's illegal." At which Albee mentions the leash law, his face inflating, rotten teeth clenched. This raises her, going from man to man, pointing her finger at their badges, shirt-pockets or lapels, stressing her dog's right to live in a free country without some beast to murder it. Winifred shifts feet, looks at the ground and seethes, "Ah, boo-sheet." Mrs. Dorsey screams, "Men like that . . ." and pauses, " . . . should stay on the reservation!" "Now, that's not fair, Mrs. Dorsey," says the Clam Warden. "The seal was minding its own business, and so was Winifred." Gil sidles over and says to her, "Don't take sides." She looks abashed, recognizing Rule #1. Lincoln winks at her. "It's not funny," screams Mrs. Dorsey. "I know that," says the young officer, "just hoping for some perspective here." Gil Amery looks to leave: "Reverend Dorsey, I can't think of anything to be done here. Please come around to the barracks if you want to press charges, if we can find the right one to press. If the seal bites somebody, then I'm bound to impound and maybe destroy it, but this is, well, I don't know, different. Maybe the Humane Society; they're in Ellsworth. Sorry for your pain. Please tell Mrs. Dorsey." Reverend Dorsey proffers his cupped palms, blossoming with wrappers. Gil walks toward his blue cruiser, its engine crooning, red light still twisting, flashing on the undersides of the elm's leaves. The crowd begins to drive off.

Winifred goes into the shop and comes out with the seal following, motions it up the plank into his truck, shakes his head and drives away, turning left, then quick right toward the bridge leading down to the harbor. Mrs. Dorsey yells, "Stop him! Somebody stop him; he's getting away! He's a devil, that's what!" Gil, about to climb into his cruiser, says back over his shoulder to Albee, "Don't know if the leash law applies to seals. Better lay low until I find out more." As he backs out, he waves to Tad and Hobby, the Fish and Game boys just arriving in their official green van. They stop alongside each other and talk awhile. Gil drives off as Tad and Hobby get out of the van and walk toward the shop, serious concern in their faces masking sorrow at having missed the action. Reverend Dorsey says to them, "My wife has suffered a great loss." Albee steps in and says, "Yeah, but it ain't the seal's fault." "They planned it. I know it," snuffles Mrs. Dorsey. "Ma'am," says Hobby, "We see a lot of animals in our job and they don't never seem mean . . . and these men have been around here for as long as I can remember." Tad looks straight into Lincoln's eyes; he weighs a hundred and fifty pounds more but is the same unusual height. "Don't know as the seal can be considered 'in the wild' at this point. Somethin' to look into. Matter of jurisdiction. Prob'ly Winifred ought to do something, don't know exactly what." "All the same, all the same," shouts Mrs. Dorsey, " . . . savages, savages . . . no regard." "Fer what?" offers Lincoln, turning his gaunt face toward her.

Reverend Dorsey, still policing the yard, whispers, "Now, now," to no one in particular, staying at a little distance from his wife, who slumps, finally crying simply, tears soaking her flowered bodice. The Clam Warden goes up and puts her long, thin arms as much around Mrs. Dorsey as she can and holds her, her hair wild now, dangling the neon rollers. Doc Perry says, "Can't be rabies; seals don't get it, though they might if they hang around enough." "I'll say," says Albee, his mouth full of hamburger. John Hutt, from the U.S. Department of Agriculture in the Post Office Building, who has been standing around looking gray, watching and listening, the quietest man in town, says, "I just don't think this is federal in nature."

Winifred's truck is outside the Lilac. Lincoln and Albee have wrestled Gooch's dryer back up the planks and laid it on its side. The seal has clambered backwards into its cave, the glass door down. Four or five of the regulars stand around watching it. The seal just looks at them. Winifred is on his stool near the bleary window, through which he can see his house across the river.

The next morning the seal humps down the ramp onto the float behind Lincoln, who hobbles along under a case of Labatt's, and ahead of Winifred and Albee carrying grocery bags, mainly loaves of Tip Top, French's yellow mustard, packages of American cheese, pounds of sliced ham and baloney, and several packs of Little Debbie's whoopee pies. The seal slithers over the gunwale and onto the cockpit floor of the thirty-eight-foot lobster boat, thunking against the pier. The air is chilled, fresh with salt and sun-ridden. Wavelets and catspaws make them squint. Lincoln has slept on board so the Buick Eight is already warm, exhaust gargling aft. He tenderly places bottles of ale in a red onion sack and lowers it off the port-side of the transom, then casts off the stern lines just as Winifred casts off the bow. Albee backs, then throttles forward, swinging her head to sea, nosing out among tethered working boats, day-sailors and a few small yachts. The bow starts to lift and fall as they pass the harbor neck and feel the open water. The offshore breeze from the southwest won't be up until after noon, so the sun is warming. A few big Atlantic herring gulls hover and sheer the wake, looking for garbage. The seal sits with its chin on the gunwale, looking out as the boat passes the #9 nun buoy while the fog, ahead by miles, backs off Cross Island, leaving it in sunlight. The dim cap shape of Mink Island emerges to the east, through the narrows by the old now-vacant Coast Guard station. The seal seems a little restless, going from man to man and then back to the gunwale. Lincoln passes a pint of Kessler and each man dumps some in his coffee mug, the pot seething on the Coleman stove bungeed down in the wheelhouse. Winifred and Lincoln start to bait the pollack trawl, shoving chunks of herring onto the hooks leadered off every three feet along the monofilament coiled into a tub. Above Mink, a few gauzy clouds with bronze bottoms and a spreading jet trail make the sky bland. Winifred signals to slow down. Albee eases back the throttle until the engine barely keeps rudder. They hear barking and coughing. The rocks off Mink are mortared with seals. Big seals, like body bags, bask on top. Mottled adolescents, in and out of the sloughing surf, wallow on layers of kelp. As the hull slides closer, this year's pups, all white, swim close and tail up in the water high as they can lift to get a look, like ivory cane heads. Albee, on signal, shifts to neutral and chocks the helm, holding the boat steady in the coming breeze and tidal current running into the narrows. Winifred slips his hands under the seal's front flippers and Lincoln hoists its rear. The seal looks back over its shoulder and, with something like resignation, gets dumped, head first over the side. Winifred waits until it surfaces a few yards off and then motions Albee to take her away, revving toward Seal Island, beyond which they will set the trawl. Lincoln draws up the red onion sack and passes out ales. The boat heaves along on the grace of the jade sea, cleaving gardens of wrack. It feels as though the surface conforms to the bottom, a brain of lobes and valleys, as if everything is finally everyone's thought. The smell of mustard overwhelms the sentiment as Albee begins to make sandwiches.

Around a wad of sandwich in his mouth, Winifred says, "She's got them New Faces talkin' to the flatlanders next door about all my machines, whole measly bunch twistin' on a rope about it. Only reason they go for that food, they call it." Lincoln licks mustard from his fingers, mumbles, "What the hell do they care anyway, goin' to Heaven soon . . . ain't they?" Winifred puts his sandwich down and quickly swerves, smoothly, to miss a drifting log boom dangling its chain. He tosses his empty overboard; it bobs away.

Because the Lilac is closed on Sunday, they take the Rim Road late that afternoon, past the old Baptist Meeting

House, oldest in the county, 1812. A crowd of New Faces in pastel suits and dresses, children looking like bouquets, mills around outside the double doors near their cars. Reverend and Mrs. Dorsey are on the steps, shaking hands with the emerging congregation. The meeting house overlooks the inner bay, toward town upriver where the Machias and East Machias merge through a series of opposing granite thumbs. Westward, the forests and bogs of Washington County steam under the season's higher midday sun. The New Faces beam upon one another. It is their last day in the old building before moving into the new brick church in town that has more room, loudspeaker systems, offices and a schoolroom in the cellar, a "bunker" as Lincoln calls it. The boys drive on by, slowly.

At Winifred's house they sit on the porch as the slanting sunlight comes under the eaves, heating the teal clapboard behind their backs. Winifred says, "It ain't breedin' season, so that won't hold it." Lincoln looks up: "You think seals are anything like human bein's? They say porpoises are." "Ducks," Winifred pronounces, as a family of New Faces gets out of a powder blue Cherokee wagon and steers each other into the restaurant. "Ever eat there?" asks Albee. Winifred stares at him. Lincoln says, "I had some tomato soup with bits of crab and scallops, but all I could taste was tomato. Seven dollars." Winifred says, "They prob'ly never ate seal...or moose." The river, down some since early spring, moves heavily. Custards and sodas ride the surface under the bridge where pigeons roost, burst out in blue puffs, then back again.

Saturday morning, they back the truck to the one gate in the chain link fence. They rig planks. The first load makes it up quickly; they take turns walking and wheeling machines into order, then haul them up onto the truck bed by pulling on the horns of the dolly. They received notice on that Wednesday. Albee came into the shop palming a steering pump as if it were a donor's heart. The bracket was cracked. But Winifred pushed the writ across his oak desk and said, sneering, "Them machines is clean; don't let cats in 'em. And every damn one works . . . now. Better'n people pay their bills."

Winifred slowly drives the first load in the direction of the harbor, the truck teetering a bit under the high-piled load as Albee and Lincoln follow in the pickup. Lincoln asks, "Suppose he's headed to the dump? Or we gonna make a reef?" Albee says, "Read somewheres they make good reefs. They use cars in Haw-y-ee. Get rid of 'em. Whole bottom's a dump by now anyway." But Winifred veers off the tar and up into the yard of the old meeting house. He gets out and drops his tailgate. "He's gotta be kidding," says Albee. They get out and walk up to Winifred as if to object. Winifred stops working long enough to say, "Them Faces ain't here no more; they's into the new one . . . looks like a firehouse. Junior says I can rent this . . . just yesterday, and I called Walsh, too, you know, he's Passamaquoddy and went to Harvard and all. He called the Baptist Society in Omaha, found out the meetin' house never made it onto their list, so Walsh called old Foss of the Congo church who runs the hysterical society and everybody says the building belongs to the survivors . . . that leaves Junior, out in New York State, now Mary Tabert's in the nursing home with that tumor in her head, and Paulette Pilchard died last winter. You allus could tell when she was listenin' in, damn canary in her kitchen. Anyways, I asked if I could use the building for a few months, maybe more. He says, 'Hell yes, the Nazarenes had the place free for three years.'"

When they open the double doors, the draft hurtles up the spiral staircase and blows a gust of noisy starlings—just up from the south and settling in—out into the air above the road. Fascia boards way up there have twisted and rattled loose on the hand cut nails. Lincoln says that in other years a pair of Cooper's hawks nested up there in the belfry, hunted the cemetery for moles and mice. Albee says he'd seen pigeons there before that, but raccoons cleaned out their nests. The sailing ship on the weather vane steers into a stiff easterly that whiffles under their trucks, around the few grounded machines and grave-stones, squirreling baskets of plastic flowers here and there.

By noon the next day, Winifred's yard in town is bald and the meeting house yard mobbed with machines yet to be taken inside. Winifred has already installed his steel frame bed, mattress, and formica table, a few bow-back chairs, the La-Z-Boy recliner in ruptured black Naugahyde, two boxes of Harlequin romances, his TV set and plastic trash bags full of clothes, all arranged in the back of the building to the west of the double doors and around the big, hot fifty-gallon drum-stove that takes a three-foot log. There is a stack of heavy wool blankets from his logging days. And the smell of moose, stewing in tomatoes, onions, two cinnamon sticks, and Old Duke red wine.

The three of them walk around out back of the meeting house and stand on the cold, mossy slope to look down on the marsh and bay, where ducks used to fly in by the hundreds, and at Pot Head, a hundred-foot-high granite drumlin with a few wind-bent spruce leaning out over the water on the cliff end where eagles used to fish. Albee says, "Somebody's gonna build up there someday, wait and see." Lincoln says, "Summer place, maybe restaurant." "No water up there as I know," says Winifred, "gotta be a forty-foot cross with lights."

Later that week, the seal makes it again across Route 1, lays curled by the shop door when Winifred comes in not long after dawn. Baited with a peanut-butter cup, it clambers up into his truck bed and Winifred drives directly to the meeting house without opening the shop. An hour later, Albee and Lincoln show up, having gone first to the shop. The church yard is bare; all the machines have been dollied inside. The white oak benches are stacked along the wall to one side and at the back of the dais under the sign that reads "Obey Thy Parents," the lettering under glass in black-outlined gold festooned with faded pink roses. Winifred stirs the pot on top of the woodstove, where he has welded a flat, braced plate of Cor-Ten. He stirs with one hand and holds a paperback in the other. "Round back," he says. Albee and Lincoln follow his waving romance novel outside. On a flat spot on the slope, in a cluster of pitted marble stones, Gooch's big, gray, speckled dryer lies on its side, ramp down. The seal is off to one side, basking in the short grass and low-bush cranberries and moss near a pan of fresh ale-wives, so far untouched, the run in full tilt. As they approach, the seal rises, swivels and backs into the dryer, starts the drum moving, slowly, then faster, its head swinging too, but in the opposite direction like one of those kitchen clocks, a cat's head going one way, tail the other and eyes rolling in between. They go back up the slope and into the meeting house. The seal follows, hunching along. Winifred is in his recliner, reading and smoking, the TV on with the sound off; the seal hauls near to watch the moving shapes. Winifred hacks, "Don't know what's goin' on in that fool's head."

The meeting house looks like a discount appliance store. Albee says so, and that Dorsey is going around talking up a storm of sacrilege and national treasure and local heritage and "all that crap because they never spent a cent to fix it up, even re-nail the clapboards, never mind replace the north sill." Winifred says, "Don't matter. They're buggin' Junior, something about a church bein' a do-mee-cile or business. Gettin' another writ. Shit, as if their church ain't business." The seal weaves in front of the TV, watching superheroes battle a big, blue, stone devil.

On Sunday they meet for noon dinner at the meeting house. About three, stuffed on teryaki moose strips and moose pot roast cooked in homebrew and cranberries, Winifred drives Albee and Lincoln to the shop, Lincoln crouched on the truck bed behind the back window. In the lot, Winifred opens a paper bag and gives each of them a sweat band and a long gull feather to stick behind an ear. Starting out the side door, Winifred breaks into a slow, lopey figure eight, arms swinging in some sort of propitiation to the sky above the Quonset, his back bending and lifting. Lincoln and Albee follow his lead, Lincoln doing crazy variations on his crazed legs. The Dorseys on their porch, reading the paper and rocking, spring up agape. Once back inside the shop, Lincoln hangs on the vise, wheezing. He chokes on laughter. Winifred sits down on a steel plate suspended on saw-horses, his head between his fists, heaving. Albee scuffles around, finishing his dance.

Next morning, Chas. O. Walsh calls Kidder's Florist to ask on his clients' behalf if the shop's customers could somehow be advised not to throw used plastic flowers and styrofoam baskets into the alders behind the graveyard, but to take their refuse home. Kidder is a Dorsey-ite. "I'll do no such thing," he says, "lots of people use the bushes." That afternoon, at the foot of the graveyard housing seamen, captains, children dead of whooping cough by the dozens—dating back to the 1760s, when King George III granted the peninsula to five of the families buried there, along with their descendants and all the later generations of other families in the town—there appears a two-by-four plywood sign, black letters on white: NO DUMPING. Dorsey, next morning, goes to the town fathers in City Hall. Mrs. Dorsey yaks at every yard and garage sale all week, saying the church is being turned into a zoo with that seal in there. And Winifred chases away two kids with a BB gun who peppered the sign. One pellet pocked Gooch's dryer. The mayor, Gooch's brother-in-law, tells Winifred confidentially in the Lilac that he sees the fun in it, but the sign is a bit much, too many New Faces upset, though yes, most of them are "from away." Especially bothered are the Geralds, an old family whose little Star Rose was buried just last fall, aged eleven months. And Junior out in New York State just happens to call to ask how bad the belfry is leaking. Winifred tells him that he's rolled a Maytag ringer-washer under the drip, that he rolls that to the door when it is getting full and lets the hose drain down the steps.

Then a few days later, in the evening, Albee and Lincoln pull up into the yard after a day of hauling traps, the old, chalk white building silhouetted against the final burn, the orange aura westward firing the yellow and green stained glass windows in front. Their headlights flare up on a bright yellow, two-by-eight sign above the lintel of the double doors. Ragged red letters spell out REFRIG- ERATOR CHURCH.

They get out of the pickup, shaking their heads, go inside. In the gloom, some light comes through the west windows, as if the glass were pink marble. The machines on the floor shimmer, float. The back rows are upright freezers and refrigerators, like closed, skeptical elders. In front of them, families of obedient top-loaders, washers and dryers mixed in with chest freezers, all with their hatches open. Down in front, three rows of front load washers and dryers, portholes in rictus, seem at the height of a hymn. From some of these mouths, faded plastic flowers hang in ecstasy. Scattered among the congregation are a few avocado and coppertone appliances. On the dais, under OBEY THY PARENTS, the NO DUMPING sign is propped on a stack of benches.

Winifred pulls up, his blown muffler cannonading. He carries in a case of Dawson's Ale, slides it in a staunch

Amana in the back row. He goes back to the truck and carries in a sort of welded hat-tree made of rebar, something like antlers. He walks past Albee and Lincoln, down the narrow center aisle between machines, and stands this icon on the oak table centered on the dais. He drapes it with fan belts sprayed with aluminum paint, uncoiling from a Shop 'n Save bag. Then he walks back down the aisle and turns to view his work. Albee scratches his ribs, thinking, asks, "Will it work?" Lincoln leans on a coppertone freezer chest. He shakes his head, smiling. Winifred says, "Walsh says all we have to do is sign some papers as members." They crack Ballantine ales. Lincoln says, "Like we was a one a' them cargo cults from *National Geographic*. Some brothers saw a plane for the first time and thought it was a god dropping stuff. Boxes of K-rations, Spam, Garands, ammo, a jeep with side-mirrors, all on one parachute." "Maybe," says Winifred. Then he says to give him a hand and they go outside and drag Gooch's dryer along the mossy grass, then bang up the stairs, over the sill and down center aisle. They turn it on its side to the right of the center table on the dais, porthole open. The seal has followed them in; it struggles on stage and looks into the hole, swivels and backs in, starts the drum swinging; it has developed a squeak not unlike the high notes of the old pump organ, its bellows choked with mouse nests and candy wrappers. The three men settle around the formica table near the woodstove. Albee grins,

"Well, you got a tax-free domee-cile, Pastor." They think about asking for donations but rule that out as against their religion. They talk about a pool table but can't fit it into the rites. Lincoln says, "We got a holy seal. I think you're beginning to look a little like that actor Anthony Quinn that time he played the Pope." Winifred likes this; he's seen the one where Quinn plays the crazy Indian chief who rides his horse in city traffic. Outside, a few cars can be heard passing, their lights flaring in the windows, then dark again. Winifred adds that Walsh said that the meeting house overlooking the marsh, Pot Head where the eagles nested, and the river might be said to have "religious significance" for Passamaquoddies. Then added, "But we ain't got a word for refrigerator."

Next morning, Winifred pushes open the doors of the Refrigerator Church and lets the spring air and maritime light flood in. Lincoln and Albee are unloading cardboard boxes of wrapped deer and moose, sliding the heavy boxes into the building and beginning to unpack them into two chest freezers plugged into the back wall. Most of the meat is roadkill, Winifred having an arrangement with Gil Amery of Troop J to come when called to clear the road, in exchange for which he gets the meat. More often than not he comes with big Mike, who moonlights with a tilt-bed automobile carrier. They simply winch the carcass up onto the tail of the bed behind the wrecked car. Lincoln drops a package labled "MINCE," and the seal pushes it around with his nose like a white hockey puck. Klein walks in with his grandson Murray, who works part-time at the Humane Society. Winifred offers them cups of Red Rose black tea. Klein shoves his glasses back on his nose with his index finger; the boy stares at the seal in front of the TV, watching Rooster Cogburn and Katharine Hepburn grunt and squeak at each other. Klein says, "Heard you were doing strange things out here…sacrificing seals and eating them, thought I'd drop by and see." Winifred grunts. Lincoln says, "You joinin'?" "Nah," says Klein, "What the hell is that thing on the table? You makin' fun of my menorah? Needs candles." "How 'bout you," asks Albee of the boy, who shrugs. Klein looks at Murray and says, "Don't worry, you aren't Isaac." He steps forward, waves his hand over the congregation and asks, "How much for the lot?" Digging in his pocket, he withdraws a wad of bills with a rubber band around it. "One thousand cash? Done?" His glasses slip; he pushes them back up. They slip again. The boy has stepped to the seal's side in front of the set. There is a shootout and horses are running every which way, making terrified sounds. Albee looks at Lincoln, then at Winifred, who says "Fun's over anyway," taking the roll from Klein's hand. "Good, that's good," Klein says, "I'll pick them up soon, got a salvage buyer in Portland." They shake hands. The boy, on his way out with his grandfather, stops and looks at Winifred. "Mister," he asks, "is it true you welded on the A-bomb?"

Winifred looks straight at the boy. "That's true, only I didn't know it at the time, Boston Navy Yard, and they know'd they could trust me." Klein says, "Old stuff, Murray. Let's go." Albee, shaking his head, asks, "What kind of church we gonna have now?" He walks over to the seal and squats. Winifred says, "Look, you really want to tell every damn fool comes in here all summer all about it?"

A few days later, the machines gone, the building mournfully empty, the floor strewn with plastic flowers, the seal shoveling around among them as if looking for something, Albee asks if the sign outside has to come down. They load Winifred's furniture into the two trucks, the seal on the mattress under the hat-tree still draped with fan-belts—wedged between the cab and one of the freezers that has meat in it. Lincoln rides in the La-Z-Boy and Albee follows in the pickup with the cooler chest full of alewives on ice. The Dorseys' car is gone when they pull into the yard in front of the shop. The seal goes under the bench while the three men move the argon welder nearer to the sliding door in front, leaving just enough room for a vehicle to get by. The furniture and the bed go to the rear of the shop, near the oak desk and woodstove. They plank the freezer down and plug it in by the vending machine outside the door. Winifred insists that the TV and the big gray dryer stay in the pickup. By now Albee and Lincoln have learned not to ask.

Early next morning they all meet at the boat. The seal slides from the pier into the cockpit with a thump. They pass the TV aboard and put it in the wheelhouse. Then they shove and walk the big dryer to the edge and lift it down onto the deck. Albee asks, "You gonna have a burial at sea?"

They chug out past Yellow Head, tonsured by a ring of wind-stunted spruce. To the north, Chance's Island with the big summer home and miserable rocks on the narrows' end. Southeast over the starboard bow now, Foster's Island with its chartreuse field, gold stone beach, tall flagpole and Old Glory waving above the camp that Gooch lives in year round, now that his laundramat is sold to the same folks that run the gourmet restaurant. Gooch never takes down the flag at night. "What's wrong with night?" Winifred asks. They ride into the slick just leeward of the reef, cut engine and slide up onto fine beach gravel. The hull whispers to a halt. Albee jumps down off the bow and receives the carefully passed TV, which he carries, struggling in sand, up to the grassy bank. Winifred and Lincoln push the dryer over the gunwale into two feet of water; Albee hauls it up the beach a ways. Then the three walk up to the camp. The seal watches from the stern, then slips over the side, slides in and waddles up the beach after them.

Gooch is at the table in the center of the big front room, whittling a decoy out of a pine block under the one bright bulb dangling on a wire over the middle rafter. On the table are an open can of sardines in mustard sauce, a baked bean can, a can of brown bread, a can of soda and a can of Holiday pipe tobacco. The floor is deep with shavings. Black ducks, mallards, larger oldsquaw, small whistlers, buffleheads, huge eiders and oversized Canada geese hang by their necks from the rafters to dry. Paint cans of all sizes and colors are strewn on the sinkboard alongside jam jars and tin cans bristling with brushes in turpentine. Small rafts of ducks paddle here and there on the floor and every other surface—two chairs, a long sideboard, and the window sills. The cot in back has a pile of ducks, colors all roughly natural: iridescent greens, blue chevrons, bright whites, all with the same orange glass eyes. Gooch, a small, wiry man with a stubborn face, smiles to have company, barely. He never meets the people who buy his ducks, some of them hunters, others for their mantles and tables. Klein buys out his entire winter's work every June. Winifred, first through the door, says, "Brought your dryer," and after a handshake and greetings all around, "and a TV." Lincoln goes out and carries the TV inside and puts it on the floor among some unpainted ducks. Gooch thanks them, says, "Prob'ly get some sort of picture over water, long as the generator keeps up." After small talk, they all go outside on the porch. The seal is in the dryer. It starts the drum swinging. It has lost its squeak. Gooch laughs out loud.

On the Fourth of July, after supper, everyone is in the Crocketts' driveway, lighting firecrackers with butane lighters and tossing them—especially the kind that squiggle around and snap in the dirt, preferably near the ankles of the women standing around, who jump back to enjoy their disapproval in a loose ring. The kids set off rockets that shoot way up, burst and expire, bits of paper falling around them and on the road like thin black snow. Some of the fireworks whistle so loud that people hold their palms against their ears. Mildred says the cows aren't going to give milk for a month. Ev Crockett, Winifred, Junior, Albee and Lincoln stand back by the shed, sipping vodka and Diet 7UP from paper cups. Some of the young fathers compete with their children, boys and girls, lighting and tossing firecrackers into the ring. Dogs and cats are long gone—under the shed, in the house, off in the woods. Grandmothers clean up the kitchen with the windows closed. As the supply of fireworks dwindles, the explosions come more and more judiciously, and as everyone tires and starts to gather the children—stubbornly hunting for and trying to light the duds—to get them to the cars, there is an enormous WHUMP from across the marsh and up the hill a half mile away, toward the meeting house and cemetery. In seconds all see the stained glass windows aglow, as if sunset had hit them, then a flare sixty feet high consuming the belfry. Every man runs for his vehicle. Winifred, Albee and Lincoln take the two chainsaws and fuel cans, several axes and shovels from Ev's shed and run for the truck.

It is eight minutes before the first fire truck comes by, wailing, headed for the cemetery road. Then two more, from Machias, and later tankers from Cutler Naval Station. Fire chasers park every which way in the graveyard; gravestones are snapped off in the hurry to see. All the water in the tankers is hosed high onto the sides and roof of the building, but the fire is mostly inside. Then it is eating the asphalt over cedar shingles, sending up black smoke in the otherwise white billows, eating pine wainscoting, hemlock studs, hand-hewn beams and cedar clapboards, the flames finally leaping out into the air as if looking for more. In two hours the whole structure has fallen in on itself, the last of the flaming pyre visible eight miles to town. At dawn there are still some thirty people hanging around, strolling the edge of hot ash. Some talk about how their parents went to Sunday school here, some their grandparents and others before that. At one point, three porcupines scuttle out from under the building's crawlspace, down through the crowd and across the road into the alder and hackmatack. There has been much to admire in how the leaded glass folded like lava over the windowsills and the tin ceiling melted, and how there wasn't a sign left of the oak benches, oak table, or dais. The big brass chandelier is a black octopus. But the best part was when the bell, its cradle chewed to weakness by flame, crashed through the belfry floor and easily through the flame-feathered second story, hitting the ground through the main floor and throwing volcanic ash and sparks high into the general conflagration. The bell sits now in a smoking heap like a Navajo oven. Stubs of smoking sill beam and twisted sheets of the pressed tin ceiling show here and there on the earth returned to flat. As the sun rises, many who have never climbed the belfry for the view see for the first time the marsh, Pot Head, the vast inland barrens as they were before the church was built.

Winifred pokes around and finds the cast iron door to the otherwise mangled barrel stove. He taps it with the doorknob he has also salvaged. It rings true, so he puts it in his truck. Lincoln and Albee are in the graveyard with others, looking at scorched marble gravestones closest to where the building stood. The Sea and Shore Warden, in her green uniform with red-lettered badge, reads some of the names aloud. Reverend and Mrs. Dorsey and some of the New Faces of the Nazarene group on or near the granite steps that lead nowhere now. Cars jockey out of the graveyard and slowly, as if in deliberate procession, steer up the road toward town.

As fall comes on, plows with broken blades, hydraulic lifts with bent cylinders, enormous rusty claws from pulpwood loaders gather in Winifred's yard outside the shop door. There are also broken and bent sleds, drags and chain gear for the winter scallop season strewn about. Winifred works long hours now. Long, carbon steel pliers in one gauntleted hand, incandescent welding rod in the other, he hunches over the slow, fiery seams. Finishing one, he straightens, raises his visor, watches the seam darken into a gray welt as if he doesn't know or care what it is he has welded.

Albee and Lincoln help part-time, fish the rest. At night, driving by on Route 1, heathen and faithful alike pass without much notice the tall, dormered windows of the Quonset hut within which vague figures sway, weaving in carnival light.

JUST FOR EGGS

They stood to bury Sam in the hilltop cemetery above Woodruff Cove. The marsh was at half-tide, the tidal brook serpentine through brown, frosted eelgrass. He had died in time to get him in the ground before it froze. Esther, a school chum, talked about Sam in the marsh, the black ducks he lugged back, hung by their necks with a cord, and gave away. She remembered his old Remington 12-gauge pocking away just after dawn. The Ghanaian minister, rich in oratory, invoked Sam as a boy, sculling his canvas duck-boat in the drift of life, borne by the tides of Christian love. Esther, Ellie's half-sister, had come from her kitchen to stand in the near winter sunlight of the graveyard. Ten feet from her car, she wore her lamb's wool slippers. Mike thought her ankles looked like stacked English muffins. The two women hadn't gotten along because they disagreed about Sam. From the first, Ellie had been so strict. Sam wasn't allowed his friends in the house. She hated rough talk, boots and alcohol. Their daughter Eva, down from Belfast, fussed with the plastic flowers, her hands fluttering over Sam and Ellie, buried to his left. She ignored Beryl, buried to his right.

As Mike walked out of the graveyard he looked east into the adjacent blueberry field, now strewn with straw to be burned off come a dry March day. Burning always brought the charged green. The big boulder was always there, gray and something like a half-buried skull. The urge to drink wafted through him, as it often did when something in him sought consolation, whenever a floater of self-pity blurred his sight. He hadn't had a drop for three years, not since the judge ordered him dry and he started AA. He was thinking about the last time he saw Sam alive.

On the ivory metal stand by Sam's crib, a ginger ale bottle, cloudy with a blop of milk, the only food he'd taken for days. Sam was curled up like an ancient dog, bony hip ridging his blue Johnny, one pink eye turned up, lids wrinkled. His liver-spotted hand flopped at the wrist, so weak that he had wrapped his fingers around a bar. At the door, Mike waved "so long" and looked down for a moment at his boots, waterproofed with engine oil. Sam waggled an index finger. His throat had closed.

Hands in his pockets, Mike went down a corridor tart with Lysol, past an old woman moaning in a wheelchair under an orange and brown afghan, then down one flight of stairs and out the ramp into the sunny lot where his wrecker was parked. Some of the residents, in wheelchairs or seated on the broad bench by the side of the building, several smoking, waved. He thought that he might have known some of them, sometime. And that Sam was just about done with making the living feel better.

And he thought about the afternoon last spring when Sam had sputtered up the hill from his house, in his 1950s Willys station wagon, and parked in the graveyard to mow his plot.

Sam rolled the mower down two planks off the tailgate and pulled the cord, then mowed in and out to either side in a small blue cloud of exhaust, around the wrist-thick poplar tree and the rose bush with the tight, hardy white blooms that Ellie always called "cemetery roses." From on top of the boulder where he sat smoking, Mike watched Sam hand-clip along the base of each stone and then rake the clippings and take a basketful to the edge of the blueberries and dump it. Sam put the basket down and walked up toward him, slowly over the uneven ground.

"What brings you 'cross river? Nobody comes over from there unless they're laid out," Sam said, digging in his overall bib for his pipe.

Mike looked dolefully at Sam. "Sam, Joanna wants to have this baby and get married. Hell, she's near forty years old! And I'm sixty-two. I got kids!"

Sam smiled, stuffing his pipe. "Just a pup."

Mike shifted his sore butt on the boulder. "Goddammit Sam, this is serious."

Sam pointed without looking in the direction of his finger. "See that telephone pole? Beryl went out to her Polara, that green one, just for eggs at Clark's, them big brown yard ones she liked? Asked me to go, which I never did but this one time. Just for eggs. Well, she all of a sudden veered off into the ditch and smack into that pole. Scars still on the pole. Pitched sideways into my lap when we hit and that was that."

Mike knew he hadn't finished, having heard the litany before. And he knew about losing a wife.

"Least it wasn't like Ellie, all radiated up like an old shoe at that Leahy Clinic. Then drowned in her own water; couldn't keep her pumped."

They were quiet for a moment. "Besides," said Sam, "you've weathered more."

"You know, Sam, there's about thirty thousand dollars in outstanding bills owed me in this town."

"You're too obliging. Those seem to have money for other things. I seen them at the Red & White...beer and snacks, steak for god's sake. I know I don't owe you nothing."

Mike nodded and looked down over the graveyard, where the Machias and East Machias came together to make a slate-colored broad that narrowed between Pot Head and Featherbed Island, then opened again beyond the marsh. The sixteen acres of eelgrass were turning chartreuse in the falling light, tide down, so the mud took on the purple sheen of sweat-soaked harness.

"How's the jeep running?" Mike asked. "You know them old Willys are getting valuable. People want 'em."

Sam waved and started back toward the Willys. "Still needs a muffler."

Mike slid down the boulder face and went along to his wrecker. Over his shoulder he said, "Hell, Sam, I'm a jailbird! No kid wants a father like that."

Sam waved his pipe over his shoulder without looking back.

The night in question was the day of the parade. Shriners from around the county had arrived with their white drill rifles, plywood scimitars, fezes and Arabian Nights pantaloons, and beaded vests decorated with moons and stars. Mike thought of himself as Cornel Wilde in his getup. In fact, he looked quite a bit like Sinbad in the mirror. Except his skin was garage gray, pores smoked by exhaust and cigarettes. In red and gold they did close order Zouave drills, quick-step shuffles between the curbs of Main Street, which was really Route 1.

Some of them rode tiny motor scooters, two-wheeled and three-wheeled, a few fitted with wings to look like cartoon airplanes. They rode with knees akimbo. Mike was in front of the marchers, barking orders the way he did on Thursday afternoons at the roller rink before the kids came in after school with their rock music. Sam always broke from sweeping to smoke and watch the six or seven local Zouaves trot in their suits or dungarees until the kids' whistles and hoots drove them home.

That day Sam was sitting on a folding chair on the sidewalk in front of the pharmacy, wearing his forty-year-old black suit from when he was First Mate on the Governor's yacht. He was in a row with residents of Maywell's Nursing Home, people he'd gone to school or crewed with in the old days, though he was still living in his house, managing his garden and keeping the house shipshape, even polishing the exposed copper water pipes in the kitchen that ran behind and over the 1918 Glenwood range he'd bought new.

Most of them were in wheelchairs, attendants ranged behind them, smoking and talking to folks with their kids and grandkids. Sam's thin hair was combed back straight over his nearly translucent skull. His forehead was green because he was wearing his poker eye-shade, his cheeks flushed from the pull on the pint of blackberry brandy that he bought every week. He held a little American flag on a stick. His glasses kept slipping down his long nose, so he'd push them back up with his finger.

The front of the parade came to a halt at the hardware store, its pots and pans glinting in the window, the plate glass mirroring flags, backs of heads and kids on shoulders. The high school band held their trumpets, flutes, clarinets, drums and tubas at order arms. Mike gave a left-face and the marchers faced the curb. Mike took up a white, plastic, battery-operated bullhorn and announced what an honor it was to have Sam there on the day that marked the holiday and Sam's seventy-fifth year in the Order. Mike came over to the curb in his blinding outfit, the tassel of his fez hanging in front of his steel-rims. Winking, he stuck the seventy-fifth anniversary diamond pin in Sam's lapel. He stood back and saluted. Sam saluted back. His hand shaking. Mike proffered the bullhorn to Sam, but Sam waved that off, said, "What a hell of a getup."

Then the drill team did a smart present arms to Sam, who saluted again. People along the sidewalk applauded and the band, in maroon and white with yellow Bulldog stencils and insignias, took up a squawky "Stars and Stripes Forever," following which the whole parade did another left turn, Mike running to get in front of the Zouaves but behind the scooters and planes already doing slow figure-eights, and wound back up Main Street to a school march, vanishing across the mill bridge, the music dying, souring out over the town.

That night, still in costume, Mike, his sons Little Mike and Lot, and some of the other Zouaves, with a few of the town guys, drank in the back room of the Texaco station where the poker game had been going on for thirty years. They were waiting to go to the Lodge where the women would be serving a baked bean dinner. Some were too hungry to wait and raided the avocado-colored fridge for baloney and American cheese with French's yellow mustard on Tip Top bread, washed down with Pabst Blue Ribbon. The sandwiches were like folded dishrags. Teeth cut perfect crescents. Mike and his boys drank Wolfschmidt vodka with the green and silver label from paper cups with Canada Dry tonic. Sam came by, still in his suit, having hidden the pin in his pocket to keep off notice; he "checked his hand," though he hadn't played for months, smoked a pipe and drove off home.

Lot, whose Harley flathead was parked just outside the plate glass front window, was manning the pumps in his costume. He'd insisted on riding his bike in the parade. His rumps hung down on either side of the seat like stuffed saddle bags. He waddled into the back room and said, "Dad, Weaver's old lady is out front all beat up and crying."

Mike rushed out and leaned into the blue Pinto that seemed to be in the garage every week. Her baby was strapped in back, its head drooped to the side like one of the "droolers" at the nursing home. Sam's term for them. When Mike walked back into the garage his face was the color of his vest; he drained his cup, poured another vodka and drained that one.

Erickson, whose father had contributed the poker chips, offered cigarettes around and said, "At it again? That son of a bitch. I know it was him shot Voigt's cow last summer, and the light off of Miller's cruiser. Remember when he was a kid? He shot off all the glass insulators on damn near every pole up Pitch Hill. She's a good looking woman when she ain't all hamburger."

Mike didn't speak. They turned off the pumps and closed up the station, leaving the two grimy but pleasant German Shepherds in the office. Then they all drove off in several cars to the Legion, Mike in his wrecker with Little Mike, Lot hanging on the running board. At the Lodge, Lot swilled beer and lurched around the spread, loading his paper plate, like the other men, with hot, mushy beans, steamed brown bread and pressed meat hot dogs. Offered food, Mike held his hand up like a stop sign, saying, "I'm in training." There was a telephone call for him; when he came back from the office, his face was flaming again.

After midnight, in Erickson's old pasture, broken up now by half a dozen rental trailers whose lights made up a little town far up on the hill, Mike, Lot, and Little Mike staggered on the soft ground toward Weaver's pale blue sixty-footer. Mike had parked the wrecker halfway down the hill, having come that far with the lights off in mild moonlight. The boys carried unloaded pump shotguns and Mike held his souvenir 9mm Luger. When they reached the trailer door they could hear crying inside. Mike yanked open the door. Weaver was at the sink in his skivvies, Joanna in the nook with the baby, her split, bleeding mouth wide open, her face swollen red and blue in the fluorescent light. Weaver jerked around, bolted toward the bedroom at the back. Lot shoved his bulk past Mike and caught Weaver as he came out waving his deer rifle, trying to work the bolt. Lot smothered him against the wall, the rifle and shotgun clattering off the coffee table onto the linoleum. Mike heaved against Lot to move him aside and squeezed by, pushing into Weaver, who was screaming, "Fuckers! Fuckers!" and jammed the Luger up under his chin, coughed in his face and pulled the trigger. The bullet drove straight up through Weaver's tongue and the roof of his mouth, through his brain and out the top, spraying the wall and ceiling with chips and pink spume. Lot and Little Mike yelled and jumped on Mike, who was already sagging down, spent and half-conscious on top of Weaver's jerking body. Joanna was still in rictus, her eyes closed.

The field was full of cruisers and pickups, men in farm clothes, Arabian outfits, State Trooper uniforms. Lights, blue and red and yellow, turned and flashed the whole scene. Half sober men strolled with flashlights. A few of the wives had come and were huddled around Joanna, wrapped in a blanket with the baby, others in urgent conversation. The orange and white ambulance, its back doors wide, already held the black, zipped-up body bag. Mike was in the back of Miller's cruiser, handcuffed to the screen. The trial months away.

People talked and gestured in the foyer and on the steep wooden stairs, waiting for a chance to get into the courtroom that had been in continual use since the Civil War. Newsmen had to wedge their way up. Some said if Mike hadn't been drinking, Weaver would still be alive and doing it worse. There was the baby to be considered. The DA's office was flooded with letters, almost all in support of the defendant. The newspapers preferred the phrase "the killing" as a euphemism. No one talked out loud about murder, despite the indictment. Weaver's ailing mother said nothing and stayed home that day, minding the baby. A moan passed through the crowd when Mike was sentenced to five years for second degree homicide. Joanna, in black, wept; she'd come to show her support. No one spoke of this as indecency. Word went around he'd be out in two. After all, he was also the town constable and dog-catcher, voted in by citizens and debtors alike, as Sam had said, somehow equating Mike's actions that night with the "free" work he'd done on their cars. Mike, on the stand, simply said he didn't remember a thing about that night. But he kept contrition out of his face. His lawyer said alcohol was Mike's enemy, that once he'd gone to the Red Maple Inn for the paper, that Lot had found him five days later in Schenectady, that he didn't remember that "adventure" either, which drew the only laugh in court that day, stifled quickly by the Judge's look. Tom, who often watched, but was afraid of gambling, had never held a poker hand, testified that Mike was loved by everyone in town, that he was trusted. People were a bit leery about Tom being on the stand; he was said to be a hippie. His wife was "nice."

After eighteen months, Mike was released on probation for good behavior. He hung up the duck, deer and bear pictures he'd learned in "re-hab" to burn into pine boards when he wasn't washing dishes in the medium security wing. Some customers bought his art to be associated with his notoriety; others in guilt for unpaid bills. But Mike wouldn't sell the ones he liked best, especially a framed one with a mallard hanging in a retriever's happy mouth. Joanna came to shellac the surfaces and backs to prevent wear and warping. When she came up pregnant, Erickson talked about bull-sperm in the freezer, referring to incarceration. No one said a bad word about that, either.

Before he had waved goodbye to Sam at Maywell's, Mike sat at the side of the crib on the steel stool, talking about his and Joanna's baby girl, her son by Weaver, other things in town, about Sam's house and how his lawn was all mowed by the Dell boy, the cemetery plot clipped by Esther herself, even Ellie's side. Mike had tinged the glass of warm milk with blackberry brandy, but Sam didn't take any. The growth in his throat had completely stopped his speech. All the attendants and nurses said that Sam was starving himself, that it wasn't unusual. Mike thought he wasn't sure that that was possible at ninety-three.

Mike said to Sam, "You should see the Willys. Lot cut all the rust out of it, cut out the dog-legs and replaced the rocker panels…no Bondo, all 12-gauge steel like the old days, and all repainted the original gray, same color as battleships. Course he doesn't fit in the door, but he likes to show it off. I tuned it, new points, filters. New muffler, too."

Sam blinked, motioned with his red eyes toward the kids' magic slate that Esther had gotten for him at the Downeast five-and-ten, the kind where you lift up the top, clear plastic page and the writing or drawing underneath disappears so you can start all over.

Mike laid the slate near Sam's face so he could see. Very slowly, the yellow wooden stylus clamped in his quivering fingers, Sam spelled out something in a childish, wiggly script. Mike looked hard, said, "Sam, I can't make heads or tails of it." Fumbling quickly, with a tearing sound, Sam lifted the plastic sheet.

ANTI-FREEZE

The yellow backhoe shivers with strain, biting and lifting half-thawed soil, spicules glinting in the bucket. The engraved stone is already in place, name and dates only, cement for the footing mixed with anti-freeze to let the base cure in the cold. The family has had to wait to get this young father into the ground, the body frozen in a cheap coffin a few miles off in Harrington's municipal cement mausoleum. With elders deceased this winter. His black F-150 pickup is parked in the shade of the 1812 Baptist meeting house by the graveyard, the building a gray-white, wind-mottled witness, sullen and disused. Vacant for years, it is more an avatar for the East Side of the river than it ever was. Fishing has been bleak, stocks depleted, like the congregation. Lobster prices to the fishermen meager. Color springs from faded and fresh plastic flowers in plastic baskets, some tied or wired to the stones to keep them from festooning the woods below the cemetery when the Northeast blows hard. At the edge of the trees is a NO DUMPING sign in red on white plywood, to stop citizens from traditionally heaving their worn-out flowers, baskets and torn flags on sticks in under the trees on Munten land, especially on Memorial Day when they "dress" the graves. The town fathers in the village across the river, Congregationalists, ordered the sign with, we "Eastsiders" are sure, comic intent. The sign now peppered with birdshot. The backhoe, having made a neat pile graveside, moves off like a praying mantis into the alders on the other side of the church road, to be picked up later by truck and flatbed. The grave will be filled by hand. Some real roses and glads are piled and ready to strew on top of the mound that will settle with spring into summer. Cars come flashing up into the pot-holed lot. They look in their rear mirrors to prevent knocking over stones. Several are prone already, where beer-drinking kids have tossed their empties and condoms on summer nights. The first to approach the grave is the Methodist parson from Millbridge, the Baptists having closed this meeting hall back in the late fifties when the flock declined to four. The dead man is the son of one of those last to go to Sunday school here, the body driven in the old ambulance, hand-painted black, that Bennett's funeral home uses for the poor and for rough roads to rural graveyards. The newer Cadillac hearse remains garaged for better occasions, for the graveyard across the river that looks more like a golf course. Maybe twenty people are here, men wearing dark, zip-up jackets, a few with neckties, others in clean work clothes with doffed caps despite the cold, a few shirts stitched with names: Tart's Lumber, Frito Lay, USN, Red Sox. The women wear plain dresses and puffy parkas, some black, most pale blue. Two men smoke back by the side of the church behind a Crown Victoria with a hang-nail bumper. One is the dead man's brother-in-law, who takes from the front seat a Wolfschmidt vodka bottle, turns to the wall and swigs. Passes the bottle. He wears his black cap with *DD-844, USS Perry* in gold lettering. Both men take a last "sip" and toss the bottle into the back seat. No one seems up for talking. There are complications. The parson calls with his arms and hands and fingers to have all gather by the grave. He beckons the wife forward and by him. She is quite fat, insulated in a brown housedress with no jacket or hat. Canvas sneakers. She is blubbering and shaking her head. The parson and the assistant from the funeral home grip the folds at her elbows to steady her, as she seems near to falling forward onto the coffin in the hole. Steadied, she continues to quake, perhaps from cold. The brother-in-law removes his cap, stares into it, stuffs it in his armpit, comes forward and gives an impatient eulogy, reading a shopping list of the dead man's organizations: U.S. Army, National Guard, American Legion, Bell's Harbor Clammers and Lobsterman's Coop, graduate of the town's high school. Basketball player. The parson senses that everyone wants this done with, so his "dust to dust" is quick. No mention of the dead man's three DUIs or that he continued to drive without a license. Everyone knows him, a hellraiser from Day 1. His wife was voluptuous in high school. She has a wide, pretty face, pouty mouth. Her gaunt mother holds the hands of the two children across from her by the grave, a boy and a girl leaning against her arky hips, three and four years old, the kids shivering and looking around without comprehension, with feral eyes. The group breaks up after the first shovelfuls are tossed onto the casket lid with a thump. They head to the cars and pickups, most left running, heaters on, without much talk. Cigarettes are lit. As the cemetery empties, morning comes to the full. Across the bay the sand road begins to glow, ends where the old pier used to be, its pilings rotten stubs at low tide. Anyone who wishes can gaze across the bay at the white trailer by the gravel bank, where the card game came to an end when crazy Jasper fired his .357 Magnum into the husband's face. Blood on the kitchen wall and spattered on five, ten and twenty dollar bills scattered on the floor, collected as evidence for who knows what. Closed coffin. Jasper is in jail still waiting for trial, pleading insanity, the town itself a case of "involuntary" everything. Jasper, in fact, was seen yesterday at Samuel's dentistry, in an orange jumpsuit, his wrists joined by a thick black electrical tie, his ankles manacled. Getting fitted for a set of uppers. This has people conflicted about the "system" to which most of them subscribe, so many in town on food stamps and ADC (Aid to Dependent Children). Some people still like Jasper, always fun. Children all over the county, they say. The swollen wife's face is bright red. She ushers her two kids to her mother's dirty yellow Subaru Loyale, gets them to climb in back quickly and slams the door so hard that the window glass crazes, but holds. To her mother she snaps, "Take them to your place. Keep them!" She puffs up and heaves herself into the F-150, starts it up with a backfire, gnashes the gears, jams into second, bucks and chews gravel too fast down the slope, bounces out onto Church Road, straightens and roars back to where it Ts on Route 1, south to Boston or north into Canada.

ACROSS THE ROOM

My room opposes my parents' bedroom. Laying there in acne, my mind's imagery is a replay of the eighth grade baseball game I pitched that afternoon against Pinardville. We lost 0-1 even though I gave up just one hit, a low fly dropped in right field that rolled all the way to the fence and scored a fast kid from first, my second walk of the game. I stew about things.

My eye catches movement in the glass of the picture of my grandparents on my bureau, a reflection of my blond, blue-eyed mother preening and swaying, naked in her big mirror. I know my father lies there, watching. I ought to avert my eyes; I have never seen her pink breasts with the bright aureoles. The mirror cuts her off at waist level, so I am spared what in retrospect would have made me fearful, the blond grotto I came out of. The light goes out in their room. I have noted the angle of the picture on the bureau.

One night in the cellar with my father at one end of

the workbench. He has taught me to use a vise, electric drill and coarse sanding wheel for making a bullet form for fishing plugs. I can hand sand them fine and paint them, using the drill for eyes and treble hooks. I am cutting a four-inch dowel from a stripped, dried pine branch a little more than an inch thick when there is motion outside the narrow cellar window above my head. Dungaree legs and sneakers go by slowly. I go up the stairs and out the open Bilco doors, walk quickly around back of the house and then to the side facing the mowed field. Peering into my parents' bedroom is Nokas, the right fielder I have known and disliked for years because he is a Greek and my father doesn't like Greeks, himself an immigrant, but not Greek. A surge of righteousness fills me. I charge at Nokas. He bolts for the wire fence, is half hiked over when I bang my right fist into the side of his head, catch his ear and knock him down. He is up and away in the dark so fast that I stop on my side. My father shows up. "What's going on?" I drop my shoulders and hands and point into the dark, say, "I thought I saw something." I walk past him as he stares at me.

Nokas quits the team. His father thinks it is all about girls. He complains about that to Coach. My righteous hypocrisy holds, but summer, even baseball, feels dull. The neighborhood is coming apart. The war with Japan is ending. Some of us will be off in September to St. Joseph's High, others to Central. Catholics and Protestants. To play baseball and basketball against each other, according to my father, who was once a semi-pro pitcher for the Lowell Sun. For him, that is what high school was for.

We never talk about college, though I am a secret reader with a flashlight under the covers. Two of the kids are off to prep schools, one in Massachusetts and another north of us in New Hampshire. Barbara, a near neighbor, is moving away; her father calls her "precocious." I had to look that word up. Too many boys in our spread out, half rural neighborhood. She taught some of us to French kiss in a game of Spin the Bottle at a birthday party. Though she is almost buck-toothed, she is pretty, a buxom vision in my wet dreams and private relief.

I adjust the picture, once, when it has been shifted in dusting. My mother removes it without a word. She tells me, years later, "You were a sneaky kid."

#2 IRON

The bags are heavy, waxy leather; the clubs wood and steel. I am thinking of quitting because of the tempers of the "fathers" who play, who call us "fuck-offs" and "dumb-bells" when we can't find, immediately, the balls they hit into the roughs, especially if they are pre-war rubber, hard to buy anymore and expensive. The synthetic balls are "duds" they hate to play with, "offing their score." Or because we caddies have slow going under those bags, on the uphill fairways in the heat. I am twelve and big for my size and my father tells me: "Watch these men, how they talk to each other, because they are 'leaders.'" The one I complain most about he calls a "hard-hitting, aggressive businessman." I feel his expectations. He says that caddying is good training.

I am half willing and half aware of something else I can't describe about this game. I like the whack when the driver hits the ball on its tee. I like watching it fly as part of my job, and being ready with an iron for the next shot.

Not too much guessing on my part. But there is something about the aura, the energy these men put into chasing and hitting a small, white ball. The manic, whispery nature of "putting." "Right on the money," they often say as the ball travels to the hole. That word, "putting," is a trivialization of something that is trivial, a game on huge acreage that used to be woods or farms. Not that I can express that at age twelve, though I do know that I feel that I come from a lower class than these golfers, who play with clubs and have a club, a clubhouse with a nineteenth hole to finish their bonding. It is all exclusive, the spiked shoes with tassels. The voice of the game secretive, priestly, full of homage. Or spoiled and bitter about a ball's lie.

But now it is night and my flashlight, with wax paper wrapped around the lens so the hard beam won't scare the "crawler" and make it pull back down into its hole, sweeps slowly on the green. I step as carefully as if I were trespassing, see a "crawler" half out, lean toward it and quickly pick it up between thumb and forefinger, careful not to stretch and break it as it gives up its length bit by bit and comes free of the earth. I pick a dozen for the Mason jar, half full of grass clippings to keep them damp for tomorrow. Then I will take the gluey mess, my rod and lunch on the first morning bus halfway to the lake and then walk two miles to Deer Neck Bridge to fish for bass, maybe perch or a pickerel.

I know my way back to the neighborhood off the

course without light and am dawdling along when I think I hear a familiar voice. Closer, it is Nana's hoarse screech that I have put up with for all my years, but there is something different now; I pick up my pace, not running but heading toward an ancient sound I do not understand tonight, not having heard it for maybe a year. I have stopped being a boy? Her voice, but for something else.

I have heard my father and mother trying to talk beyond Nana's presence. She will leave for Finland "pretty soon," live out her life with her five sisters, one of whom is a Major in the Salvation Army responsible for connecting hundreds of Holocaust survivors with relatives in the U.S. and Canada. I will never see Nana again. None of us will, says my mother. Nana's husband, Johann, died when my mother was twelve of silicosis and pneumonia, contracted during three years in an Estonian labor camp run by Russians during the last years of WWI. For being in the Finnish underground. They talk about Nana, honoring how she studied and learned English but turned on them by supporting Roosevelt, especially Eleanor, her deity. "How come," my father asks my mother, "Edit hates Russians but is a Bolshevik like Roosevelt?" I liked the sound of the word "Bolshevik." It was like the name for a breed of dog. Borzoi. But I could picture that dog. Edit Suontakanen from Hanko, where Mom was born.

Closer to the lights down our street, off the fairway, I hear her wailing sporadically in English. "He's dead," she cries, "He's dead." Her "change of life," though I don't know what that means, makes her crazy, according to my mother, so I think this is about Johann. She has nightmares about tomatoes chasing her down the street. As I come in, my parents lead Nana from the front porch, and when I get into the kitchen through the back door she is still riled, wagging her head from side to side, my parents stepping back from her, palms up and toward her, saying, "OK, Edit, OK." She quiets when she sees me, then steps to the hallway closet where the laundry hamper is, and my father's golf bag. Returns to the kitchen light, a sturdy woman in a green housedress and clumpy 1930s shoes, her legs wrapped in Ace bandages. The Mummy. Her face, though, is like Tonto's, high cheekbones, black hair pulled back very tight into a bun. Her mouth is tight as she goes back out on the front porch in the yellow bug light and jams the end of the #2 iron, handle first, into the old, corroded flag holder facing the street. To the head she ties one of my father's long black business socks that dangles in the night air amid flickering moths. Quietly, she says out over the street, the houses across, the golf course, "Roosevelt is dead." Turns her back and staggers to her room in the back of the house, muttering in Finnish.

THREE-POUND HAMMER

I was working for the City in the summers during college. I drove a steam roller over svelte asphalt in new suburbs when not pushing wheelbarrows, raking and tamping to make driveway inlets. I swung the three-pound hammer, cutting edges while focusing on not taking off the fingers of Stu, my pal holding the chisel upright. I would not hold the chisel. I was a promising pitcher. I got away with that. My boss had three digits missing, about which he was phlegmatic. He told me, first time, holding the chisel himself, "Keep your eye on the chisel head and hit it. Don't think." He drank at the American Legion, for whom I played. Schlitz. Our high school basketball team also practiced and played games in the gym there. The school's "band-box" gym was too small. Girls played there. Sock-hops.

One morning, a little before dawn, my mother woke me up (she'd never ask my father, who had to be at the office by eight, I to work by seven) pretty much squalling that "Tweetie," her huge Siamese, had broken a screen and jumped from a second-story window. I rose and without coffee walked the neighborhood, ran into a guy also half awake who said there had been a hellacious yowling, so I guessed that Tweetie had been out fighting and fucking all night. When I ambled back to the house I went by dull instinct back behind the attached barn and found him in the corner of the little slate-walled garden, swinging his head and moaning, totally stoked on adrenaline. So I pulled on my heavy machinery drivers gloves, coarse leather with stitched canvas cuffs that I stored over my belt, and approached him, saying nice things and, stupid me, reaching. He sprang on my right arm, raked a fine vein open over the cuff and bit through leather into the knuckle of my index finger. Fifty years later I can trace the scar, the white line. My mother arrived in her pink chenille bathrobe and the cat leapt up into her arms, having spent himself on me. I said, "Ma, you gotta have that cat nutted." But she had turned back to the house with her favorite child. I went to work, my arm wrapped tight in peroxide-soaked gauze and Scotch tape. At lunchtime I stopped by the clinic and got a tetanus and antibiotic shot and real bandages, having heard that cats have mouths more toxic than dogs, or human beings.

Two evenings later, my father drove into the barn, opened the car door and dandled his leg with the sleek silk business hose. Tweetie lit into that leg, raking and biting as if it were a promise he had made to himself. At seven that evening, the cat went to the vet and endured the humiliation most wished on others by certain of our own species. Thereafter, for years and years, I did admire that cat, his agile stoicism and remove, especially when he sat on the porch post and leapt on any neighborhood dog to ride them from the yard. Nineteen pounds. My mother could not diet him or he would kill the chipmunks in the garden wall. Bring half a squirrel onto the porch as an offering. That cat had it made. He died in the laundry basket, in the small room inhabited by the hot water tank and white machines, while my mother was away visiting a grandchild she didn't much care for. I was on leave from the Navy and watching the house. My father too had died. The next morning, after laying the cat out in the sun for a while, in state on the porch, I buried him in the backyard by bordering laurels—dug a decently deep grave and set him to rest in a khaki duffle bag. I made a white pine marker. When I had to return to DD-844 the day after my mother returned, I suggested that it was a temporary marker until she selected what she wanted . . . or let it go. The day she died, years later, she asked the ceiling of her room for help. I said to her doctor in the hallway, "Doc, I wish we were in Amsterdam." He replied, "Or Oregon." He upped the morphine and she was gone at 7:22 that evening. She never trusted me.

CANARY IN THE KITCHEN

The telephone lives cradled in the dark, behind the gate-like doors of a small hardwood cabinet in the kitchen. If Tom happens to be in the house and thinks it likely to be his mother when it rings like a fire bell, he shifts to the table with his coffee cup crooked on his finger and pulls out the chair nearest the phone, opens the doors and picks up the phone. If not busy, he does this carefully when it isn't their house ring and listens in, at least briefly, to see if anything interesting is going on. A party line on the dirt road down the peninsula fingering the Bay of Maine. All eight parties, not all at once, listen in—a sport, often to distort what they hear, grist for more humor. Tom and Lee, his wife, hope their own conversations are private. Their phone is modern, with a round dial that spins and clicks when dialed with one's forefinger. An ugly transformer can hangs high on a pole nearest the tar road, a mile from their Victorian, hemlock Cape. Many of the old, blue glass insulators have been shot away by ambitious kids with .22s. But old-timers like Sam, next house down the road, remember when the line strung on those insulators was a 12-gauge soft-steel wire and the company left a roll of it for neighbors to patch the line with in winter, when sub-zero contraction and wind broke it, leaving the wire dangling. By twisting the ends together, having added a piece, and leaving it stretched along the top of the plowed berm, "service" was maintained until spring, when the company would do a proper job. Sam said that kids took care of this temporary measure and one time held hands to see if talk would travel through their bodies. Swore it did.

Tom and Lee know when Paulette Pilchard is listening in because she has a canary in the kitchen. A wild but communal song. Paulette is like a switchboard operator, constantly plugged in. Reputations to be made or tainted. One could die established or disestablished. Egos could be seared, poached or reheated. Lee and Tom are pretty much aware of their vulnerability when the phone rings for them. They tend to talk to people "from away." Exotics of high interest. A world beyond. No one tells Paulette to get off the phone; she supplies everybody with eggs.

One warm, bright morning Tom picks up the phone on his ring and it's Betty, who will with ease jump into any private call with an opinion. With no greeting she says, "Eb says the damned calf's fell in the cellar hole and he can't get it out." She hangs up.

Tom knows he's the one to have been called because he's nearby and likely to be home—Lee teaching fulltime while he takes care of an annual flock of sheep, a beef critter, the woodlot, the gardens, the greenhouse and other work, like mowing, that needs to be done if they are to keep up affectations as back-to-the-landers. He does some substitute teaching to stay respectable and make a few dollars. He is sometimes called a hippie. But by bartering lamb, some wool, salted sheepskins and sometimes boarding someone's beef or horse, they are tolerated. Fishermen like meat, bring halibut, scallops, or mahoganies, the thin shelled cherrystones in onion sacks. Sometimes Tom trades for welding or engine repair. He brings a carcass once the weather's turned cold, or a hindquarter, hangs it in someone's cellar or shed and forgets it. No words spoken, the rear universal seal for his IH Travelall gets replaced, or seafood shows up at their place and a home-brew or two get quaffed. Tom feels, more than less, real.

He parks at the double-wide and walks down toward the cellar hole where Eb stands by, smoking. Why nobody rebuilt there after the fire that took the original pre-Revolutionary War house can't be imagined, because the slope faces the bay and takes in sunrise and sunset over water. Locals seem to hold to notions of special places, or people, being "bad luck." So maybe that was that and a shame because the original granite cellar stones were placed by an artist, in line, true and locked. Tom could build on them tomorrow.

The cellar hole holds a nice patch of red raspberries, partly sprouted through a tossed bedspring. It's said the Glenwood parlor stove was overloaded with the draft too far open on a sub-zero night and turned pink. The door warped and popped open, spewing embers, with the children asleep upstairs in two small bedrooms, each with the atypical addition of a dormer.

Tom and Lee would never sleep above a woodstove. Their Victorian Cape has high ceilings, with a steep staircase to the upper rough chamber. They use the traditional Cape-style main bedroom downstairs off the parlor where one of their stoves, a Yotel, works. Their Rottweiler, Toby, sleeps on their queen with them in full sense of privilege.

When the Sullivans' lace curtains and a chair fired up, their dog woke them by barking. The parents bolted upstairs to get to the children, just before the stairwell became a blowtorch. They pushed the kids out of the dormers to slide in the snow down onto the less angled back porch roof, slide more and drop off into the forgiving pile below. "Father" and "Mother" followed. No one died, though "Mother" landed on one of the girls, sprained her wrist. The story also has it that before the whole building became a conflagration, "Father" Sullivan managed to let the crazed dog out the front door and drag a parlor rug out onto the snow, where the family and a few red-faced, gaping neighbors squatted on top to watch the house subside noiselessly in flames, sparks and smoke, under a black sky crowded with stars. Could have been a picnic; it was warm enough, for a while. There were no phones to call the fire house. Just flames seen from upriver. Too late, too far to run to the rescue. Next morning, curiosity brought a wagonload of the curious to the extinguished site.

Another version has it that Sullivan's still in the cellar blew up, the fire burning down into "the prettiest blue flame." Tom likes that poetry.

He feels momentous in approaching Eb. He is by happenstance being included in the history of a famous cellar hole. Better than a grave. He feels significant, though he sees himself a wan prospect for local history, being "from away," "not from heah." He enjoys responding, feeling needed and potentially heroic, as most men do, and when he nods at Eb and Eb nods back he clambers down into the hole, about five feet down but not close to the calf, so as not to excite it. A Holstein, light boned, not solid bodied like his annual whiteface Angus "beef critter," and it seems quiet as Tom steps carefully around the fertile bedspring, a shot-pocked washtub, some rotten boards. The calf, which as Eb says has "stopped bawling," lets him smooth his hand along its back, used to being handled in the shed. Male, a meat animal. Lean, not fatty meat.

Maybe eighty, ninety pounds. Might go two hundred and fifty by next year. Arms under its waist and chest, Tom takes a big breath and exhales, then lifts. Heavy, but he gets it up high enough for Eb to help a bit by pulling the front legs. Eb is on his knees, his face flared. The calf bawls into it. Tom pushes its bony rump up over the edge. Eb rolls with the calf, who gets itself up and staggers, trying for elucidation. "Stupid," growls Eb, as he struggles from his knees to his feet.

Tom steps up gingerly on the edge of the washtub and hauls himself out while Eb gets a loop on the calf. They trudge back up to the shed where its mother is tethered in her stall. Blue milk, not good for butter, but okay for drinking, like skim, for coffee and Betty's perfectly crusted donuts deep-fried in lard. Eb is puffing and Tom worries about the exertion, Eb's chronic atrial fib and occasional angina. Eb will not go back to the doctor. Or take "rat-poison" blood thinner, forgets his daily aspirin. Lee has listened in on him complaining to his daughter-in-law, who lives across the bay, about heartburn and being out of breath. Angina can feel like that, often self-diagnosed and dosed with Tums.

Eb asks, "Take a sip?" This is an event. Shared success among men. Tom revels, though he puts out cool. There are two aluminum folding chairs with gay plastic strap seats, so he sits down while Eb opens the rusty fridge door and takes out a bottle of Smirnoff, pours two foggy water glasses half full and passes one. They sit, don't say anything for a while, realizing they haven't much in common, until Eb says, "Early spring." Tom tries to be as terse. "Lettuce up in the greenhouse." And, "Damn dog eats the tops off asparagus shoots out back." Eb, "Them crowns was set a long time ago. Good patch, allus was. Used to get some, near all summer." Before Tom and Lee bought the place, which had been up for taxes for six years, the cedar shingle roof leaking and rotten, horsehair plaster ceilings here and there pee stained, one long section of the cellar wall fallen in … too many ill-fit stones responding to frost, breaking the mortar, the house unheated for years. Tom reroofed with green asphalt shingles and rebuilt the south side foundation with cinder block.

Sam listens in, maybe to Paulette, who knows everything. When he wanders up to the house from his, because he is in love with Lee and can always get a homebrew, he sits in a wicker chair in the kitchen and stretches out his long, bowed, sea-going legs, stuffs and lights his pipe, and settles in. Aromatic Holiday tobacco. Never overdoes his stay, though. All Lee has to do is stand up and stretch and he gets the message. This time he has to tell Tom, "Heard you lifted that steer out of the cellar hole like nothin'." This pleases Tom no end. He preens, as if looking for a kiss. Lee yells, "Oh God!"

One morning Tom walks with Toby down to Sam's stout Cape, in the Ames family since 1743. Walk-in fireplace, three-sided with Dutch oven. Though Sam uses a kerosene "pot-boiler" all the time now. In his late eighties. The sliding woodshed door is open, as is the inner screen door faced with nearly opaque plastic sheeting, for wind, Sam claims, so Tom can see straight through to where Sam is standing at his kitchen sink, brushing his dentures, his tan wall-phone cradled against his neck and ear, wire dangling. He waves his brush to signal quiet. Tom stands there until Sam softly puts the phone back on its cradle, rinses his "teeth" and puts them in his mouth, pats Toby on his wide skull. "Yak, yak," he says, "all's they do, all about nothin' t'all." The "steer" story is stale, no new context. Tom is mildly interested in buying Sam's dead second wife's Dodge Polara, under a blue tarp in the backyard. Sam has his venerable Willys wagon.

The year after he lifted the steer, Tom pastures a Holstein named Bobo. Nobody else wants a Holstein steer, cheap at auction in Bangor. Bobo has wide horns and is playful, will charge the two of them and sheer off at the last instant. Tom carries a stick to wave him off, Lee prepared to jump. This one time he comes at them and hits, slips on one of his own recent wet flops, "meadow markers," his legs going every which way and his whole bulk landing on its side, hard enough to disgorge with a guttural whoosh its whole first stomach full of glutinous green grass. Bobo gets up clumsily, shakes and looks satisfied. This is a fine laugh; the hotline picks it up when Tom reports the comedy to his mother.

Tom ropes Bobo up from the pasture to the front lawn and tethers him to one of those ground screws that are really for big dogs, or a sheep. For Toby when young, before he gained trust about running off. Just strong enough to hold Bobo on a twenty-five-foot chain.

Bobo is overall amenable, if occasionally antic. Tom goes out after supper in his shorts and flip-flops to shift the tether to fresh grass. Bobo has chewed down a nice circle. Tom bends over, counter-clockwise unscrewing, and when he looks up, by instinct, there is Bobo's lowered head coming at his, butting Tom's hard enough to send him staggering back, shaking to clear sparkles and a profound, sudden headache. Eyes cleared, enraged, insulted, Tom steps forward and kicks at Bobo, driving the ground screw between his big toe and the next one. He hops and swears and howls, soaking the sandal with blood. He scans, furious, for a hammer, an axe, a board, anything he might wield, then hobbles to the kitchen door, howling for Lee. Who looks out the screen door, howls back, "Oh God!"

Next day Mac comes from the store where he has a real butcher's counter, meat wrapped in white butcher's paper and cotton string, the price penciled or felt-penned on the paper. Mac pays Tom fifty cents a pound, which they estimate at $185 for Bobo, trucks him off in a horse-trailer.

Hamburger. Lean steaks. Medium sized roasts. Soup and dog bones. Lee says, "It wasn't Bobo's fault!"

Mac makes a story of it that runs the line. And Tom has tried to make a joke of it to his mother, about limping and his bandaged toes that won't fit without pain into shoes. Tom thinks a little self-deprecation never hurts, and maybe expands his image. Makes him human, for a stranger. He feels somewhat lucky because Bobo keeps alive, by association, his reputation as having lifted a full-sized steer from Eb's cellar hole. Bobo could have been that calf, the one Eb got rid of. Tom never tries to set the story straight. Or embellish. He leaves that to bored others. Bobo is now part of a local serial, dragging Tom into the footlights. Lee looks away, aggravated by Tom's needs. He says to her, "You have no sense of humor." She does not respond.

Private house phones, cell phones. E-mail. Abstract issues of privacy. Party lines a thing of the past, locals meet each other, accidentally on purpose, often in the new Shop 'n Save. They chat at the Chevron station. They are very slow to adapt to their children's methods of communication, fingers too stiff to "text" on the miniscule buttons. Too much magic to simply "swipe" to receive or send a call. Mac has closed down, what with competition from the chain store. Betty and Eb die. Sam dies. Tom and Lee go separate ways, Tom hanging on for a year, then selling their house to "summer people." The Sullivan cellar hole

has berries, the bedspring and washtub. Paulette lives on.
No bird sings.

GLORIA ARTICHOKES

Lee stirs and yawns, her long legs kneed to the IH Travelall's dash. "Close yet, Tom?" To check if I'm awake …a good thing. This two-hundred-mile round trip, same old Route 9 from Wesley to Bangor, is getting old, though this time, on the way back, we'll continue east through Calais into New Brunswick to Deer Island.

"Watch it!" she yells. The doe clears the windshield, then leaps the guardrail and vanishes down the bank into the woods. So fast…I could not brake. Had the deer been any slower or lower… "Well, that was lucky!" "I'd say," she says, and we lapse into silence. I'd been daydreaming. We both know that Dr. Duffy doesn't elicit luck or any lightness of being, just stagnancy and hope, compounded by the situation ahead on Deer Island and my too mild interest in our immediate "project," what Lee expresses as "male indifference." I don't like being categorized; it is too convenient and makes me fear what she is thinking but not saying. Men hate exposure. The prospect of Deer

Island is more depressing. A dead girl.

I still have the harmonica, a Hohner G, in the glove compartment (saw it as we left, when I got out my sunglasses) . . . played low . . . my imagined, sentimental Russian melodies, that belonged to my grandfather in Finland. Nana hated the sound because the G does sound Russian. Though she claimed to have been a distant cousin to Nijinsky. Madness. The G sound suits my still likely melancholic reveries that Lee says I have to "manage," "let go of," if we are going to "do something." I know she means that I have to learn to be less phlegmatic about family.

She handles the bills. I find it pleasant to mow endlessly, or trudge along behind the Troy-Bilt tiller, or nail row after row of new cedar shingles to the north wall against winter. I reshingle the roofs of the house, shed and barn with green asphalt shingle from Canada. I am good for that, for steering my boat between hundreds of happy lobster buoys to find my own, hauling my few "pots" in light fog, watching them materialize from the depths full of strange life, strange every time as if for the first time. I won't "fish" with wire traps, love the old-fashioned half-round, water-logged "pots" made of lath. Heavy to haul from the bottom, the water hard to see through, like fog on the bay. I need some obscurity, cloud, gist, haze, veil, dim movie, whatever. It is why, I think, I easily move my body to the rhythms of rural work. I write a poem about it.

MILKING

In the darkening barn, one bulb stares, flyspecked.
I squat the stool, press my brow to her loin.
She moans, already dripping in the pail.
I inhale the ammonia of hay and urine.
It doesn't clear my head. Instead, a foggy, white river
winds through a cheese-green valley,
grass still poking through the snow.
My hands mope between my knees, my eyes closed.
I rock my head against her meat.
She moans again, so my hands begin to work,
slow pistons shivering a hill. We heat.
I bleed this river into evening. My sweat
blends with slick where she has mopped herself.
Our teeth grind. Someday I will leave her hide
draped on the fence for birds to hammer the fat.

We stay awhile, lovers who have been considerate,
now spent and listless. As if she wouldn't start
to eat all night, suck gallons of the darkness up.
As if I wouldn't try to sleep and see,
The rods and cones beneath my lids
firing in their little baths of acid.

Complaining a bit, but I like to feel resigned. To not
be able to do anything about anything. An understanding
of the world. If I retell in company my "big eel" story, Lee

proposes I have a Freudian "thing." A submissiveness she calls "obvious." When I ask when she might quit condescending, she says, "Eventually." And laughs, punching me in the shoulder. But I tell it anytime. It goes like this:

My black, hand-painted '38 Plymouth sedan sits roadside, cooling, off the dirt and gravel road. The brush strokes show. I hide the key in a magnetized metal slide box and stick that under the fender. I could lose the key in the woods or river. With my rod and bag I pick my way the quarter mile down through paper birch and popple to the wattled beaver dam that births the Union River, brown and falling a few feet from the foggity base of Great Pond. I teeter across to the far shore gravel, unsheathe and assemble the nine-foot Montague bamboo fly rod, the one I bought with money made from caddying and selling golf balls that I hunted for in the roughs and by wading in the pond, feeling for them with my toes. I thread the floating line and nine feet of transparent leader through the guides and tie on a big #2 Eagle Claw hook on which I skewer a dervish night crawler, picked from the damp paradise of the church lawn the night before. There are no trees left along the far shore, just druidical stumps of hemlock and spruce. The back cast is free to run back in the air, then whipped forward, up into the current, funneling to the dam. I let the worm bottom out and roll, hoping a big smallmouth will inhale it.

The swinging line stops dead. A snag? There are sodden pulp logs on the bottom. I lift the tip of the bamboo and try to flex the hook loose, but sense slow life in the line. Too heavy for bass. Snapper? I lay the rod down on the bank and begin to hand line. I don't want to break the rod. The lilies close to shore twist into a swirling bouquet. "What the hell?" It all comes toward me hand over hand and finally, right at the bank, the big eel's head appears, sleek, body thick as my forearm and easily five feet long. Pulled, the eel swims out on the bank; the lilies swim back and spread to calm as the writhing eel makes a tortured wrap of the nylon leader around and around its gill. Nana chopped theoretically dead eels into four inch sections and dropped them in a hot, oiled pan where they would twitch and jump, spattering oil before they sizzled down to quiet. Nerves. Eels have over one hundred vertebrae.

I reach down and, as I would a bass, put my thumb into the eel's mouth to grab the lower jaw, lift the eel to unhook it. Wrong! An eel's is a "true jaw," double hinged. It clamps down on my thumb hard enough to break my nail and rip it half off, leaving me bleeding when I violently shake it loose. I take from my bag my father's Iver Johnson Supershot Sealed Eight .22 revolver, load and shoot the eel, twice, in the head. It whips. Holding the bloody leader tight, with my Ka-Bar knife I saw and hack off its grey-eyed head, which I could have done in the first place. I put the revolver back in the bag, still loaded. The body writhes. I rinse my bloody hand in the river and wind the thumb with my handkerchief, leave the eel for a coon, fox, or eagle to tear apart. Maybe mink. I take the rod apart and tightrope back across the beaver dam, climb back through the woods, start the still warm car and drive out to Route 9, the "Airline." My thumb throbs. I am afraid of infection, so stop at the little store in Auburn, tell my story to the owner-lady, buy white tape and a bottle of iodine. There is a skull and crossbones on the label. I have some clean Clam Shack food napkins in the car for gauze. Iodine stings! I will scissor the flap of nail when I get home. I could have taken the eel home and eaten it in a bloody bonding ritual, its last day and my future. I imagine it writhing in the trunk. But my mother would not have cooked it; she is rid of Nana's influence. She is an American now. Eels are European. I could have cut the leader short, tried to work the hook loose and released it. A four- to five-foot American eel can be over forty years old, surviving anything but boys. And otter. My father is almost forty, too old to be drafted. Has weaker eyesight. And children. At whom he looks myopically, doubtfully. Besides, Germans love eel. I have a daytime learner's permit to drive. School starts in a week. It is 1944 and my parents, from Norway and Finland through Ellis Island after WWI, believe this war is over. It has caught my valorous imagination. The car, my first, has a new clutch assembly that I put in by myself.

That's my eel story. I may be rid of it. Having written it.

Lee and I visit a friend in southeastern Ohio, where he teaches English for Ohio University. He has invited us to his annual game dinner. He is a fine bird hunter and serves a dozen or more woodcock, baked in red wine with tarragon because the tiny things have a slight liver flavor. They eat worms. He poaches pale ruffed grouse breasts slowly in sauvignon blanc and green seedless grapes. Braised pigeon breasts baked in brandy and canned plums. Others bring squirrel pie, rabbit ragout, and one of his fishing buddies a kettle of snapping turtle soup. I ask that guy how he catches snappers. I write a poem on his images:

TURTLE

I dive writhing and blind
in the Ohio's silty current
my hands dowsing the mud bank
Find a hole a cave
I could have come out of

That doesn't stop me from reaching in
using up my lanky air to feel her
snap on the length of broom handle I grip
while my right hand wraps her spiked tail
and turns her around
my legs pushing against the fundament

to draw her skidding and hideous
up to light

I am poor hungry and human
But that's not it at all

Lee reads this, says, "See? It's your mother!" Sometimes Lee calls me "phlegmy." She picked that word up from a fisherman's wife at PTA, talking about her husband. But most of the time she finds me just not paying attention. It is hard for her. Have I objectified her? As part of the movie in my head that I am incidentally, haphazardly making all the time? Lee says, "You and the damned eel! If you tell that story one more time! You have been bitten by your own cock!" "I thought it was yours," I say. Lee: "There you go again!" Echoing our fathers' god.

Anyway, I am driving along in my theater, and don't remember whether it is the Spanish olive or the Gloria artichoke bottle between Lee's breasts, under her favorite gray cardigan—Lee, dozing, her arms crossed, long and shapely legs stretched now in jeans, knees just clearing the dash. We have to get this jog done, get to Bangor, turn around and get back, cross the border at Calais, drive to the L'Etete ferry landing in New Brunswick for the last load of the day to Deer Island. Artichoke. I pass the side road to Great Pond, where I parked when I caught the eel, and then by the little store where I bought the tape and iodine.

I think about old Sam, our neighbor, who is taking care of our dog, Toby, while we make this trip. A long retired sea captain who worked the "coaster trade" on two- and three-masted schooners as a kid, delivering lath from Machiasport and paving stone from Vinal Haven to Boston, the East River or Perth Amboy. I imagine him most as captain of the hundred-foot, America's Cup class, Bluenose-style "yacht" with a ninety-seven-foot-high spar, owned by a beer magnate in Rhode Island. Sam in his uniform—blue-black wool pants, gold buttoned jacket and heavy overcoat with pea-jacket lapels from Abercrombie & Fitch. Sam's "boat," hauled and wintered at the Herreshoff Yard in Bristol. She escaped the hurricane of 1938. Hauled for good in '42 to have her keel, tons of lead, cut off for military ammo. Sam, born in 1888, lives down the road from our place. His house is a century older than ours, mid-1700s. One of his stories is about being eighteen years old and putting in at Deer Island overnight with eighty hogsheads of herring in the *Willoby*, one of the last herring boats left on the coast of Maine. Still had a naphtha engine. Sam shook his head and said, "That island is dry as the Congo church." But we know that every returning fishing boat and local car on the ferry from L'Etete is loaded nowadays with "supplies" for the family and friends. Machiasport is "dry" as well. A trip to the Machias State Liquor Store next to the A&P fixes that.

Now they are talking about privatizing the sale of booze, so it will show up in the new Shop 'n Save. The A&P on Main Street, which is Route 1, is giving up. We love its squeaky old tongue and groove floorboards. Its real meat counter, cuts wrapped in white paper with cotton string. Anyway, Downeast folk don't have cocktails, they drink. Sam says he's never been drunk.

This time Lee and I don't want to leave home, even for Dr. Duffy, because Vito, Father Vittorio, is arriving from Hartford. He may be at the farm already. He can let himself in, knows the routines, can work the woodstove and haul water from the hand-dug well in the front yard. He knows the homebrew is in the old Philco in the barn. He will have brought bottles of his family's wine from Treviso. He will walk down to the pasture and check the sheep, toss them fallen apples from the Antique Gravenstein just outside the gate. Vito, youngest of six boys, no family farm land left for him, no way to support a bride. He is a farmer at heart; it is what he says he really knows how to do. But he loves what he does, in "spiritual agrabiz." And he's met Captain Sam and likes him, can seek him out if he wants. I know he likes being alone on our land. But we always want time with Vito. It isn't a religious thing. He runs a big, tough, minority parish. Doesn't talk about it unless we ask. He is into the Boston Celtics, good wine and food, cooking. And the way we live pretty much off the land, blanching and freezing about three hundred and fifty pounds of greens a year. He is politically astute about this nation, compares it to Italy with its three sets of books and understood corruption, its amused pride in the Medicis, poison in the Vatican. Americans favor assassination by gun, he says. No subtlety. He loves Pope John for his liberal tendencies. We enjoy arguing points from Aquinas' *Summa* like a chess game. With "vino." Vito is in Lee's eyes always welcome because he is "terribly handsome," a "delicious waste." Of course it is more than that. Lee has a near spiritual devotion to teaching kids. They share real interest in children. Vito and Lee both dislike the notion of charity . . . a shallow motive. Republican, Vito says. Yet Lee is against socialism. Restless about welfare and Aid to Dependent Children, though she supports it as a necessary evil. I say I am exactly one third Bolshevik and no more. "Ineffectual," she replies.

We have no oppositions, ambiguities or contradictions about Vietnam. And Kent State settled our apprehensions about military collusion with the Chamber of Commerce. We have nothing external to argue about in the lives we lead. Or follow. Except what is between us, this little bottle's argument.

Lee's mother knew Vito, met him at an old age home he serviced, as she did by reading stories aloud one afternoon a week. At age seventy she had so serious a crush on him that she went by herself to Treviso to visit "his family." Lee tells Vito, "She has adopted you; I am your stepsister." Much to his pleasure.

Toward Aurora the smooth new asphalt silences road noise. Spanish olive? Or Gloria artichokes? Getting up this morning was anxious. Lee, her lovely muscular butt on the edge of the bed, me between her long legs wrapped around my back or waving rhythmically in the air, holds the sterilized bottle until I am, what, ready? The look on her face is empathetic, not a rouser. Catching the spurts a homely thing. Then she stands, screws down the lid, pulls up her panties, jeans, hauls on her down jacket, tucks the warm bottle under her armpit and heads for the Travelall. Seated, switches the bottle to between her breasts, under her folded arms. I drive, maybe the last of the several times my "specimen" has swum to Bangor and Dr. Duffy, who holds the bottle up to the fluorescent light and peers sort of myopically to say, "Good volume." We know this has nothing to do with viability. Or genetics.

We haven't said a word to anyone about this; it is the seventies and attitudes, though challenged, cling to the apparent stability of the fifties. "Sperm" is an unheard word. Unless you are talking whales. I beg Lee not to tell either of our mothers. Mine would think, "It's not his fault." Hers would ask, "Has he been checked?" And our fathers would both have something urgent to do in the garage.

One of these times, we are about to leave for Bangor, and Sam comes into the kitchen unannounced, as is his prerogative and our bane, with yet another of his "gifts," a jar of "dillies" (pickled yellow beans) that his first wife, Ellie, put up. She's been dead for a third of a century. Or "bloobry" jelly, always with a rug of mold under the lid. We dump these offerings after he leaves. Keep the jars. Sam idly picks up "our" bottle from the oil-clothed table where Lee has put it down in the warm kitchen to go to the outhouse. Sam looks at it. At me. I wrack my brain and finally say softly, "Sperm." Sam drops the bottle and it bounces on Lee's hand-braided rug. I pick it up and shove it into my inside vest pocket, go out and start the car while Lee ushers Sam out the door. Sam is ninety years old, "sharp as a tack," as they say, "quite a figure of a man." He goes off down the road to his house, rocking with the walk of a man who has gone bow-legged with sixty years at sea.

"So how'd Sam take it?" I ask. Lee takes the bottle, looks at me askance, says, "I simply said, 'Tom's always joking around. His cockroach Borax concoction.'" We laugh...a little. No one should be able to lie that well. I feel blessed. Lee says, no answer expected, "Why in hell did you say that?" I am still thinking up an answer.

The story with Sam is that a year after Ellie died, "all burned up like an old shoe" at Leahy Clinic, he'd left "the Port" and gone "up" to Portland as a night watchman for B&M Baked Beans. Tired of being alone in the house. There he met Beryl, a big, sort of rough and jolly nurse at

York Hospital, when he went in for a health check ordered by B&M. As a child, she had been Sam's very first "love" in sixth grade. But I found a picture of Ellie tacked inside a wall cabinet in his little barn/garage, along with all of his car "history" in pencil: *Oil change, Buick, Sept. 12, 1932.* Sam kept logs of weather and such all the time. A sea captain's habits. The inside cabinet door is for car service, written all around the one photograph, a lithe, not pale girl at a school desk, probably seventh grade, one long black braid hanging in front of her white blouse. I have seen a picture of Lee at that age. A match, so I understand Sam's keen crush. It gets so bad that our often afternoon lovemaking is interrupted by just the fear that Sam will come into the kitchen with his usual "Where you been?" He often wraps his long arm around Lee, the top of his thumb in the crease under her breast. He is bold about it, right in front of me. Lee puts up with it. She says once, "Look, it's not worth embarrassing him; he's very old."

Once, Sam just happens to be on his roofing ladder (inspecting the chimney, he says) when Lee goes out to take her usual summer shower under the warmed, black plastic rain barrel, about two in the afternoon. She is never modest. From that crow's nest vantage he can see her uphill above the young tree level between our houses. He has his brass binoculars from the yacht. For two weeks Lee goes to visit her parents. When back, Sam comes by, says straight-faced, "Ain't seen much of you lately."

The floating contradiction is that Lee doesn't want to sell the farm to avoid subjecting her, our, proposed child to the local customary ways that she disparages. I say, "We can homeschool. I think we can do that, what with me at home most of the time." Not really, if I worked the animals and land. I cannot keep a half-hearted tone from my voice. Lee says, "A child needs to be socialized, especially an only child. Besides, I don't want to be seen as religious. And how could I continue teaching with my own kid a holdout?" So she is planning just one kid. In part, I know I am unfair, because she seems adamant about staying. Is it for my sake? But what's fair about negotiating her wordless urge to be pregnant, to survive her husband? Here is the bottle, perfectly warm between Lee's beautiful breasts. I say to her—once—"Your baby gland is swollen." She replies, "Yes, is yours available?" She can be so physical, grabbing me through my jeans, pushing me at a wall, or couch, or bed. I'm getting stiff under the steering wheel. But I am vague about the intrusion a child could make on our life. Partly because I am male and because I less and less value our species, its necessity. O, I know the arguments: IT was put here for us. IT could not be appreciated but by us. My handball partner, who summers nearby, works for a year, every three years, in demographic statistics and planning at the Chubu Institute in Nagoya. When I stress over some environmental issue he says, "Don't you get it? It's all about human overpopulation of the earth: war, genocide, boundary and religious disputes! Cutting down the Amazon for Christ's sake!"

Lee complains that the kids of "these people," the fishermen and clammers, the workers in the salmon plant, are all doomed to repeat their parents' lives, the girls "knocked up" in high school, deserted by their boyfriends and on ADC payments within a year. I say this is a hangover from when subsistence life along the shore was all there was. A hundred years ago when fish, clams and lobster were plentiful. I repeat that these people can't afford to eat the food they catch. She mourns that so much of her teaching is for nothing, though she is popular at the school. I catch her despair. She thinks me cynical. I remind her that a few special kids do come through and get on to college. "Not the bulk," she answers, "The ignorance is overwhelming." My emotional investment is simply less. I think of the tons of salmon growing in the blue plastic cages off Cross Island. All swimming counterclockwise like everything else . . . water in a flushed toilet bowl. Maybe I am not really interested in children. I worry about her inherited patrician snobbery, think myself philosophically democratic on this and other "local" subjects. I sympathize because I think our own assumed, affected way of life is passing with theirs, honor their trying hard, unselfconsciously, to keep things as they have always been, boys impatient to get out of school and onto the water with their fathers and uncles. The fish stocks have played out. Most fish for lobster now that the cod are gone and lobsters are in abundance without their biggest predator. Cod eat baby lobsters. Prices for fishermen so low that FHA boat loans fall behind. I know fathers and boys who cannot read or write. Though their grandparents were literate. At least biblically. And newspapers. Their kids passed along through the schools. Lee and I are outsiders and always will be, even if we stay. Lee says I am "elitist." And "condescending." I see local solidarity as part of longtime survival, day to day "gettin' by." And I like being with people Lee's father calls "losers." He wanted me to go with Travelers Insurance. My own father, who was raised with this same Maine stock, grew up around and in the granite quarries on Vinal Haven, then "made it" on the mainland as a branch bank manager, ruthlessly cutting his roots early on while climbing into the American dream in a moderately priced suit. I know it is retro for us to work our old place, bought when it was auctioned for taxes: sheep, a beef critter, three gardens and a greenhouse, homemade ale, boarding horses, caught up in the "back-to-the-land" movement. But it feels real enough to me to keep to the outhouse, water from the well, wood heat and oil lamps, a windup alarm clock (though we don't need that with Toby around), to be in the moment with laborious days, axes, chainsaws, Troy-Bilt roto tiller, scythes, water buckets, our life in a still authentic place, dreaming along in my movie. Scott Nearing is an admirable martinet, a purist who doesn't get into the local thing. Lee thinks him "relentless," but an important icon. For what useful future for civilization? Any more than us? I dislike the notion of personal salvation, that virtue for many back-to-the-landers. Lee and I get by on the imperfect labor we perform. I like "gettin' by," a bit embarrassed by my pretensions to native lingo. That my father would slip back into naturally when needed. I like physical work, within which I can maunder, a would-be poet. Such a silly thing to do. Elizabeth Bishop grew sick of "primitive personalities." I suspect Frost as well. Snobs. Me too? I like drifting in a boat, or in the Travelall beside Lee. I think that Lee lives with me by love and some sad, predictive tolerance. She needs more. Tolstoy said, "If you want to be happy, be." But did he? I mean, between Nicholas' will to violence in protection of his traditional and conservative "rights" and Pierre's still idealistic interest in saving Russia by his own good will and philosophic disquisitions in the forum, I see the future as just more swinging of the disastrous pendulum, differences resolved by war and agent "heroes." I can't help being like Pierre, though I admire Nicholas' newfound strength. Lee does like to hear me talk about this stuff, as long as I don't go on and on. I remember something in Eliot's *Middlemarch* that I would not share with her: *His soul was sensitive without being enthusiastic: it was too languid to thrill out of self-consciousness into passionate delight; it went on fluttering in the swampy ground where it was hatched, thinking of its wings and never flying.*

Not me, exactly, but close; she'd jump on it. So I argue with myself, steering along this day, about my surfacing conflict with Lee's desire to have a child. Maybe men never really want to "have" children? "Who 'has' children anyway," I ask Lee. "Oh, you silly," she answers. Her dismissal does not register that she may be forming a decision. "Yeah," I think, dreaming off, suspicious that I want my lover/mother to myself. Her will is "harmonically hormonic," as she says, but I feel no urge for replication, no son to vindicate my years as a good athlete on state champ teams. What ex-jock car salesmen do to their boys. As their fathers did them. My father worked out some of his dreams on me, but he was not obsessive. He took golf seriously. Had pitched and played right field, semi-pro for the Lowell Sun team, during the Depression. Two bucks a game. I spent enough time in locker rooms. And I can't conceive how to be with a daughter, but am interested in a vision of Lee and her daughter, a center about which to orbit with some freedom toward enigma. My mother watched me as an object of bother, picked up after me before I had a chance to do it myself, which I hardly did. It felt like a truce without a battle line. She was a formal, stoical mother. While my father had Victorian fantods, she took the apparent pregnancy of my high school cheerleader girlfriend as an act of fate. I came down for breakfast and she said, "Good morning, Pop." Not the kind of humor I could handle. Fortunately, hot sitz baths or luck brought about a liberating period. I can still see the smile on her face, entering school at the girls' end way down the hall. Our homeroom teacher, Miss Sale, also grinned, looked at me and shook her head. I went my way sort of stunned, more than relieved. I had endured a mystery. The catcher on our team, a pal, went steady with Paula, the sexiest girl in our class. He said, "It's easier to beat off."

Lee will leave me because I have no place or future I want beyond what I have. I won't change myself. I am not goal oriented. I drift and work. Write some, desiring to write fulltime without acknowledging the fact. She quietly says, "You are old before your time."

I don't really like to have Lee go through another dawdling artificial insemination at the hands of Dr. Duffy, who seems to me to enjoy her body. Lee says to me, "Lookie here, the speculum is freezing and the Doctor's hands are corpsy." My sperm count is "normal," Duffy says, as usual. I find that somewhat insulting. Lee's "apparatus is all wonderful, a miracle," Duffy says, sort of waltzing around in the small white room. I think maybe the Fates are trying to tell us something about making a child. I would never claim divine intervention, that assault. Dr. Duffy works with a sort of turkey baster, is polite enough, wears no latex gloves, tells Lee "not to worry, the time will come." Every time. Finally, I can't believe I hear him ask Lee if she has tried prayer. Lee laughs, says, "No, not yet. But when I do I am not sure what I'll pray for." Duffy is baffled, drops the subject. I am baffled too. I can't get how a medical man can still think magically. I know he can't deal with Lee. The way he gets goofy in the small, sterile room with her. "Now you just lie here awhile with your legs up," he says.

On the drive back, I imagine Lee imagining life swimming into her life, the universe she is. Millions of baby eels. My mind the Sargasso Sea with its floating rafts of beady kelp. The two of us off to catch the last ferry of the day onto a Canadian island, as if into a possible new life. Lee always imagines living in other homes, too, mostly to justify the one we have, to vaguely recheck what we are doing. I am attracted to lights in any fluorescently lit kitchen, motion, specters in passing.

A poem comes from this:

DELIVERY

The amber lights of the school bus
sweep the plowed banks on turns
at four in the afternoon, gracefully.

A deer hunter, cradling his .30-30,
has left his post in the cedar grove,
trudges the berm and gets picked up.

The kids, too, are beat. A few,
given to staring out of windows
at nothing in particular, stare

where not much stirs their vacancy,
an indignant cat with vole, an ominous
bough, or risen doe, waiting to cross…

…the quiet snowing, the snug
dark under trees, the slate ice pond,
routine in this version of delivery.

He stands in front, back to the kids,
chats with the driver. His orange jacket
blazed by passing cars.

He turns, scans them.
They bore him. Everyone gets born.
He went to the school. Rode the bus.

He hasn't seen a buck all season.
Sore talk of the "way early rut,"
weather's malice. What to do?

The bus stops at tracked driveways, leaning
post boxes, old houses and double-wides,
kitchens bright as Hopper's diner,

warm with dingy fluorescence,
hard maple chairs, black plastic clock,
white sink…hung apron.

The trip now has its secondary purpose, to help with the mess involving students from a college we are some-what familiar with. The president there is an old friend, and a friend of another friend we met through yet another from associations with people in the Peace Corps... as if one thing always drives another, or is another, a self-mythologized voyage further into uneasy and comforting exile. Another reverie, I know. Lee acknowledges and gets on with things. We stop at the Airline Diner and eat huge hamburgers draped with fried onions, ketchup and a flap of American cheese. Lee says, "If this takes I won't be eating food like this for a long time, if ever."

We leave L'Etete in fog. We are at the rail, listening to the battened cries of gulls. A short distance offshore, the fog lifts like a linen napkin from a lap, and we can see the outlines of roofs, then houses on the shore of Campobello, Deer Island off to the northeast another seven miles or so in mist. Lee points to Roosevelt's "cottage"... with its many small beds and rooms for Secret Service on the ground floor to the right as you enter the Visitors door, she tells me, having been there on a class trip with her "kids." The large bay window glints under the Canadian flag. Where FDR "caught" polio in the cold water. We wonder how cold water could be a cause of polio, remembering the prohibition about swimming during our childhoods before Salk. I swam in a quarry, but that summer the town fathers decided to dump garbage down the cliff to keep us out. The water here at the foot of Fundy is so cold that fishermen never bother to learn to swim. Seven minutes and one's extremities are lead. We swam through the peelings and paper. Flowers.

Deer Island looms closer, clean, Protestant, the ferry slip a dark haven between basalt knees. We lumber conventionally into the pilings to starboard, the impact straightening our course toward the ramp, the ferry nosing in on a churning reverse engine. The crew ties up, lowers the ferry's ramp to make a bridge to the land for the few passengers and cars. Ours is the one Maine plate on board, but the Travelall, like the IH Scout, has credibility everywhere Downeast, including New Brunswick. You have to manually lock or unlock the Warn hubs to go out or into four wheel drive. Forest green is "the" color. I look down into the dark between the ferry's steel hull and the wharf to port. The ferry heaves in and back, in and back, before it settles. Something like vertigo attracts me to that shifting chasm, but this is not Hemingway's primal swamp. It has upfront energy, the Atlantic. I think of Norway. Immigration. And Finland. Sunlessness. Dire images, never having been to either.

The Roosevelt name always keys my memories of my grandmother, Nana. And one of her nephews. Gunnar and Edit were solemn, tonally secretive about Johann and his damned boot knife *puukko* that haunted my feeble romance. I was maybe eight. But they wanted me to absorb the myth. There were *nisu* and coffee and tea with milk on the table, and I the only grandson at the time. Nana would bare one foot at a time, having unwrapped the Ace bandage from her leg, soak the foot in Epsom salts in the kitchen sink pan . . . a hideously knobbed thing, bunions she'd pare with her dead husband's *puukko* as she smiled to see my horror. The skin would fall in the pan like bits of onion. I did not understand the bottle of vodka brought in from the snowbank, the juice glasses with no juice. It seemed they drank water. My mother frowned. Kept busy.

Gunnar had three fingers missing on his right hand. He told me that huge Russians caught him with a sack of potatoes he'd stolen from a truck. He said it was a mistake that they'd missed his thumb and trigger finger when they cut the others off. Months later he ran off from the labor fields. The guards were drunk. He ran to the harbor and hid in a storage shed on one of the wharfs. Finns found him. He joined up. He was fifteen. He described his white, full-length parka and white skis. His rifle wrapped in a bedsheet. Swedish Mauser 6.5x55mm. Flat, fast, universal. He could ski and shoot with that hand. I believed him.

Johann, dead ten years after three years in an Estonian concentration camp, had been a municipal sculptor's apprentice as a teen in Hanko, the port furthest south in Finland and closest across the Baltic Sea to Estonia. Four hundred and fifty thousand Finnish families sailed for the

New Land after that war, in fear of Russians and Germans. They got as far as Oregon. My father could not understand why, like Nana, Johann was an ardent socialist once in the U.S., once he got the family through Ellis Island. Wasn't it Bolsheviks put him in a concentration camp? Johann danced the tango in the Finnish Stoneworker's Veli in Quincy, built as a union hall. Where my father and mother met at one of the dances. "Veli," in Finnish, means "brother."

My Norwegian grandfather on my father's side was also a stonecutter. He never met Johann, who died at age forty-three of silicosis, stonedust in his lung and bouts with pneumonia—from work in Estonia, the dank quarries in Quincy, and fishing in winter off T-Wharf in Boston. Nana hated Russians, croned herself immediately upon his death. I loved her with some desperation, though she frightened me much of the time. She'd sit and rock endlessly, her legs wrapped in those Ace bandages, her feet stuffed in those clunky shoes. Gunnar suggested the *puukko* had a lethal history, at night. In Finland.

LIME GREEN EASY

Her lime green easy top-load with the Viking lid
on its four thin legs on the wooden laundry floor
quaked to the swishing of the agitator.

Its head a wringer, turned on, white rollers

gumming and juicing the sheets, socks, pants,
while its black gut motor hung,
hummed on the slack black belt.

The cracked cord sparked with every splash.
The dual action in the tub, the suds, the crone
standing by, red hands hanging, ready to lift the sop,
finger the laundry piece by piece, edges and corners,

her daughter's eyes narrowing to see her grin,
feed my shirt into the wringer that grabbed it,
spewed it flat and clean, down in dead folds
into Nana's yawning wicker basket.

We'd listen to *The Lone Ranger* at 4:30, afternoons
with zwieback and tea with sugar and milk in it. Later,
when I saw early TV, I realized how much she looked like
Tonto, played by Jay Silverheels. Black hair pulled back
tight, high, polished cheekbones, same shaped face with
bright black eyes. I overheard my mother say to someone
that Nana had the longest menopause in history, noisy
nightmares about tomatoes chasing her in the street. I
didn't understand the word menopause, but kept the
image of the tomato chase. Nana and I would load a red
Skippy wagon with newspapers and tin cans of cooking
fat to turn in at the market for the war effort, for which
we would get hard cardboard OPA tokens in different
colors that she put in the slots in our rationing book. I
think that if you had enough of them you could even buy

shoes. Leather went for Army boots then, so it was not easy to get new civilian shoes. I wanted canvas sneakers, surplus khaki. Had they been worn by dead soldiers? I'd slowly drag the wagon, she in her wrapped legs and heavy black coat, me in my dungarees and sweatshirt and baseball cap. I was gangly, with acne. I did what she told me to do. Her English was amazingly clear. A fast learner with a great ear, she listened to the news and read the local newspaper every day. She loved Eleanor Roosevelt. Nana passed on to me political emotion. She did not like it that I was dreamy, and was suspicious of my being out at the lake on my island, or wandering Bald Hill in the snow with my Winchester, octagon-barreled .22 short pump plinker. I think I may have sensed strife in our house, my father so determined to climb the American ladder, to reject anything about the "old country." My parents hardly seemed to speak to each other with Nana around, a numinous presence. This was not a conscious part of my existence. I was happy enough. Nana went back to Finland when I entered college. But I think my mother more stoic, having never had a childhood. She never seemed interested in mine, wanted me to "grow up."

"It would be nice if this were just an outing for us," Lee says as we lean on the ferry rail. I almost say, "Wouldn't it be pretty to think so," but manage to stifle. Instead, I whisper, "I love you." That falls so flat that I am even more self-conscious. Lee sometimes returns this loving phrase, but never offers it first, never. She is so confident, expects me to know she loves me without her having to say it. Wellesley, top of her class in Classics. Seven years of Latin. I look at her leaning on the rail and say again, "I love you," such is my slavishness. I am a creep. The urgency of Bangor and the urgency of Deer Island weigh on me. I do not like having to leave the farm at any time, but this time is too strangely special. A theater, I fear. Lee would like it to be for other reasons. Like carrying a child into a fabulous vacation for a family. I have blown it.

Lee wrote a short story and left it for me to find in the attic, when I put my heavy winter clothes away in the big moth-balled trunk after she split. Irks me that without pretension she is a cleaner writer than I am. Not even an English major. Classics.

FRESH START

Pauline brushed her flashlight at cobwebs bellied by insect hulls and soot. A pallor of sunlight hung in the window slot. She squatted on damp pea-stone at the chimney base and shoved the rusty iron plate aside, opening the ashpit. Alex had scrambled up the roof ladder in his running shoes and was straddling the ridgepole with his head in the chimney top. His voice came from way up. "Hello down there!"

She leaned to the hole. "Hello up there!" She poked

the flashlight inside. The cellar draft sucked past her arm, venting stale air to the sky.

"I see it, Lovey." His words from warmth and light tolled in the flue. "Wiggle it around." She wiggled it. "Clean enough, I guess. Looks OK. Looks good, in fact. You can come up now." Pauline pushed the plate back against the pit and wiped her gritty hands on the bricks. Loose mortar clattered to her feet.

Her flashlight beamed across a stave barrel. She walked over, raised the lid. Inside there was whitish grainy stuff with lumps beneath. It smelled sour. She poked it with the flashlight and something shifted.

Alex was at the top of the stairwell, braced in the door. "What's going on?"

"Something in this barrel. Smells funny."

He groped down past sardine cans stacked on the stairs, eyes blinking. She wiped the flashlight on her pants, handed it to him. He leaned over the barrel. "Phew. I think we've discovered Tut."

"What's this white stuff?"

Alex felt it with his finger. He barely touched his tongue to a grain. "Salt."

"Salt?"

"Something preserved in a barrel of salt."

"What?"

He shrugged. "King Tut." He knelt and hugged the barrel.

"Here, push. Let's roll it into the light."

One bronze shaft of sunlight rode a line of stones pointing to the barrel. Tiers of blue canopic jars loomed from the canning shelves. Slaves trudged through mildewed stains on whitewashed sills above the cellar boulders.

"Al, you sure?"

"We ought to find out. It's our house now."

She straightened her arms and pushed. It tilted but wouldn't shift.

He said, "Wait." He took the light and sprinted up over the sardine cans.

Pauline was alone.

He clumped back down with a carving knife. She grabbed his wrist. "Al, no. I mean, we don't know. What if? . . . What if, well . . . " She covered her eyes. Salt sifted from her fingertips. It was her argument with his father about cremation. She clutched Alex's arms on the rim.

He slid the lid back. "Of course. Never mind. We'll just forget about it. After all, it's been here a long time already."

Pauline leaned against his shoulder, watching the barrel. The chill seeping across her chest subsided. Then they turned and went upstairs. Alex closed the door, easing the latch shut.

He rolled up his sleeves to scythe spindly grass stalks for compost. In the pantry Pauline poured a fresh basin of water and pulled on her rubber gloves. Fingerprints had been locked in layers of grime throughout the house. Knees had polished the cabinet paint away, hands had smudged rings around the door knobs. Wall boards nailed above the kitchen woodbox were waffled with kindling nicks. She had been scrubbing the woodwork, doors, cabinets, scrubbing every surface until the paint flecked off. Her suds became a stew of loosened soil. She had worked from room to room. She spent most of each day scrubbing.

Early evening when the breeze subsides, and just before a rain, is best for burning. It was perfect. The woolly clouds were stitched with shiny tin piping. Alex shouldered an Indian can dripping water that trickled from under his belt down into his socks. Pauline carried a shovel and a big broom down the back slope to the cairn of gnarled alder branches filigreed with dead leaves. Alex pulled newspaper from his pants pockets. Pauline handed him her fistful of matches. She licked her finger, held it up, then pointed. Alex stuffed paper under the north edge of the pile and struck a match on a rock. Pauline stood back as the flames flickered, then rose into the brush. While the sky darkened the fire soared up, spewing fireworks of dead leaves, tinder flares. As heat torched the core of the pile Alex backed off, pumping ribbons of water at the edges. Pauline swatted her broom at the little prairie fires smoldering from flying sparks. The sun blazed into lime sky under quilts of clouds. "Look, Al. I think those are raspberries." She pointed down the slope to buds on thorny stalks.

"Hey, I think so. Oh boy, raspberry pie, jam, syrup."

"How long?" The buds were miniature berry shapes, hard, dry, straw-colored.

"Oh, couple of weeks? Keep checking them to see." Then the sun vanished behind spruce and the tin melded away, and the fire shrank into glowing coals ringed by velvet ash.

A long sedan nosed though road dust, into the dooryard. It was Lucien and Anna Hooper. Alex hailed them from raking rotten shingles he had pried off the main roof. Anna was a proper ramrod lady stepping right out of some old family photograph in her starched cotton frock and hose, with those white summer shoes you chalk from a bottle. Anna stepped through the scraggly grass clumps that Alex had tried to cut with an old handmower he'd found in the barn. Pauline came to the kitchen door. "Oh, hi." She wiped her rubber gloves on her shorts, then tore at the sticky cuffs. "Come in, come in and see how we're fixing up the house." She opened the screen door with one gloved hand while Lucien and Anna entered the cool kitchen. Anna sat upright in a kitchen chair with her hands clasped in her lap. Lucien settled into the rocker by the window. Alex grinned at Lucien's hob boots tapping the floor. He swept his arm toward the window. "Isn't that view coming along nicely? We've cleared and burned the alders and now we can see the bay." Lucien adjusted his steel-rimmed glasses to open water between pillars of spruce. "It's a nice spot. As a boy some of my favorite memories are with this old place. There's nothing like a family home."

Alex moved beside the enameled kitchen range. "Well, you can come here anytime you want," he offered, stroking the oven's chrome trim. "That's why we thought you might like some of our, well, your berries." He smiled to Pauline.

Lucien rose, hooked his thumbs in his suspenders. He rocked forward on his toes. "I brought my basket. I'll go fetch it from the car." He slipped past Alex and out the door.

"Excuse me?" Alex said to Anna, and followed Lucien.

Anna turned to Pauline. "Dear, what are you going to do with that rough chamber upstairs?"

"Oh, I think we'll finish it last, when we see how our money holds out for fixing the place up. We want to put in electricity and plumbing first. That attic is a big space, the whole upstairs, really."

"Lucien told me a man built this house for his wife. Then her baby died at early birth and she died too, poor dear, so he closed the house and left. That's why it's not finished up there."

A high whine jangled in Pauline's ears. The barrel was under Anna's feet. She saw Anna's sweet composure and didn't dare ask. The funeral home had sent that small black box that they had buried whole in the spring rains because they were afraid to open it and see what was inside. She said, "Lots of Hooper family history here?" Anna said, "Oh, yes. They moved right in. The boys slept in the attic, the girls slept over the kitchen."

"Do you believe in ghosts?" Maybe that would do.

"Well, now." Anna smoothed her lap with a gracious hand. "When Lucien and I were first married we lived across the bay in his cousin's house. I heard things thumping at night, like chopping wood, you know, and asked him if he heard it too. He always said no. But years after we moved, he confessed he'd heard it. Now I just don't know what to make of it." Her benign smile broadened. "Lucien's brother Frank never married. He lived on in this house after the parents died, tending his pet cow, who put out his right eye one day with her horn. Frank loved her anyway. One morning a neighbor found him dead right here in this chair." She nodded to her chair. "Lucien closed up the place. Then you folks came along."

Pauline swayed and grabbed the table edge. She studied its swirls of wood grain. "Then why didn't you take it, Anna, if it was vacant? Lucien loves it so much here."

"We like living in town. This is too far away. Trouble in winter getting in and out. This road is an old Indian path, did you know?"

"Would you like to see what I've done?" Here was a chance to escape the kitchen.

"Why yes, dear."

Pauline pushed from her palms on the table, stood. She escorted Anna out of her chair, into the parlor. She showed how she'd erased soot around flowers in the wallpaper, how she'd chalked fresh stripes in the front hall, and her scouring and waxing projects to bring the old floors to a shine. She showed the heavy green window shades she'd shortened and hemmed for fresh color and light. Then she poured Anna a tall glass of iced tea and they sat quietly in the parlor with their ice cubes clinking.

Voices came from the lawn. "They're back," Pauline

said, and helped Anna out the screen door into afternoon sun. Alex was showing Lucien his system of ladders and staging from shingling the main roof. A basket sat on the grass between them, heaped red with raspberries and currants. Pauline tightened. Her whole crop of berries sat in that basket. Alex helped Lucien load the basket into his trunk. Lucien and Anna waved goodbye from inside their car. Pauline turned to Alex. "Oh, Al, my berries!"

He winced. "God, Lovey, I know. What the hell could I do? He went on and on about this old place and picking and picking, stripping every branch. I couldn't tell him to stop. What could I do? What?" He followed her as she ran down the slope to the raspberry patch. It was stripped. She checked the currant bush beside the kitchen drain. Stripped, too. She caressed its leaves with a limp hand while he stood aside and watched.

Kalunk. Kalunk, clunk.

Pauline woke.

KALUNK. She lay still and heard it again, clunk. It came from the rough chamber. She fumbled in the dark for Alex.

"Al, listen." "Hunh?" He rolled away from sleep.

"Listen! The attic!" she hissed. "In the attic!"

They lay stiff beneath the blankets and listened. She was prickling with goose bumps. Alex pulled the sheet to his chin. "Jesus."

"What'll we do?"

"Wait. Wait until daylight, Love. I am sure as hell

not going up there and I'm not going to let you go. We'll find out tomorrow."

She whispered at the ceiling, "We'll wait." He cradled her and they shared warmth, lurching in and out of sleep, listening, until finally the noises ceased and it was dawn.

Pauline poured their cornflakes and coffee. "Al, Anna told me about a ghost."

"Oh, no. Here?"

"No. Over there." She pointed at the bay. He listened, put down his mug. "OK, let's go see." They climbed the attic stairs in sun glowing through windows hazed by fly wings and spider smears. In daylight the attic had no dark places. They picked their way among broken chairs, shoe lasts, crackled halters, newspapers still wrapped in twine, coffee cans rattling with sardine keys, cheese boxes of lamp wicks, casters. They opened chests, found gnawed soap bricks, coughdrop tins, chunks of beeswax. Alex turned toward the stairs. "Well, nothing. I have to get back to barn work."

"I'll stay here and sort through things."

"You scared here alone?"

"Not in daylight, I guess." She looked around.

Scuffing issued from beneath the eave. "Oh." Alex approached it. Pauline ran downstairs for the flashlight. He leaned over the unfinished wall and felt along the eave. Then he peered through a slit in the boards. "Well, well. I've found our ghost. Ghosts." From behind the lath he brought out a blinking fuzzy raccoon pup. It squealed, trying to suckle his finger.

Pauline reached out to it. "My god, it couldn't be more than a few weeks old."

Alex beamed the flashlight behind the wall. "It's a nest, and there are five, I think. Get one of those burlap sacks from over by the stairs and we'll put them in it."

Pauline held the sack while Alex put six squealing, frightened pups into it. She looked into the bundle in the bag. "What now?"

"I guess we drown them in the rain barrel. That's what they do with kittens."

She bit her lip. "I can't do it, I don't think."

"We have to, Lovey. They'll stink up the attic and chew it to shreds. I'll weight the bag with a stone and it only takes a few minutes. They're too young to really know."

Alex carried the bag to the rain barrel behind the barn. He carefully placed a stone beside the pups, noosed the bag shut, and lowered it into the barrel. Pauline watched from the corner of the woodshed, ready to walk away. There was gurgling, squealing from beneath the water. She clamped her hands over her ears. It seemed a long time before the water was still. Then Alex pulled the soaking bag up by its rope and laid it on the ground. He dug a hole behind the barn. He placed the bag in the hole and shoveled it over. "It's done, Lovey. All done."

Pauline turned into the house. She passed the cellar door and paused, then opened it and looked down to the barrel. It was still there. She closed the door and went up to the attic to be sure the ghosts were gone. She saw a large pinkish rectangle near the raccoon nest. It was a faded Bible with a broken clasp on a celluloid cover. She brushed off the dirt. The first page read *To Mother, Love Frank. Christmas 1889.* "Wow," she breathed, and turned yellow stiffened pages. A letter fell out. It was written on blue lined school paper in faded script. She unfolded it carefully so the creases wouldn't separate. She saw the signature and ran downstairs with the letter.

Alex was cursing in the dark of the barn. "You know, there was a big saw here when we looked at the house. And a woodsled, too. Both are gone."

"Some things are gone from the attic too, I think. But Al, listen to this letter I found, all right? 'Dearest Mother. I am well and working hard. I have a room over the kitchen. I work afternoons with the cattle, milking mostly and go to school forenoons. We are very busy but we rest Sundays mostly except for the milking.' You know, there was a marble-top bureau in the attic? It's gone. 'I am keeping my hours for Uncle John. He says maybe in the spring if you want to send Frank, he can make room for him too. If that would help you out. It gets lonely here. Your loving son, Luce.'"

Alex picked at mosquito bites on his scalp. "So?"

Pauline looked up. "So."

They quit work early and drank cold Bud on the doorstep in the sun, then fried cod when the breeze from the sea cooled their kitchen. Alex was rinsing dishes when Pauline rushed in the door. "There's a raccoon on top of the chimney!"

"Which chimney?"

"The main chimney!"

He grabbed his rifle from two coathooks over the parlor door. Lucien had advised he keep it loaded. He motioned for Pauline to stay inside and quickly went out. The raccoon was silhouetted in twilight, a black moon against an orange sky. Alex moved toward the rhubarb where he had a clear view in fading light, raised the gun, then centered the animal in his scope. It was a tough shot. He squeezed slowly with the crosshairs on the raccoon's head. He fired. With the explosion the raccoon vanished. Pauline came out.

Alex tensed. "I had to shoot her, right?"

"She had to go. She had to."

They circled the house but couldn't find her anywhere on the lawn. Pauline eyed the chimney. "I bet she fell down there. What if she's wedged in there?"

They went down cellar. It was almost dark now, and the flashlight cast a weak beam in the gloom. Alex opened the chimney plate. No raccoon. He reached up inside. Drips of blood and liquid were splashing into the pit, blackening the ashes. "I guess she's up there alright." He wiped his sleeve across his chin. "Tomorrow. It's too late now."

He filled another burlap sack with rocks and tied a heavy rope to it. He propped his ladder against the eave and climbed up. Pauline followed, hauling the bag to the eave. She handed him the rope and he dragged it over the gutter, up his roof ladder to the peak. With a grunt he hoisted it and lowered it into the chimney. Then he fed the bag by the rope down the hole. It stopped. Pauline shielded her eyes with her hands and watched. He lifted the rope to arm's length and let it go. He did it again. The bag of rocks tore from his hands and thundered down the flue.

They found her lumped in the ashpit under the rocks. She was very large. Her tits were swollen with milk. She had been shot through her head. Alex saw an apple crate in a corner and loaded the sticky body into it. He dug another hole beside the dead babies, burying the family together. "Al?" He turned, saw Pauline hunched with her arms across her chest as if to protect something weak inside. "I wanted a fresh start, Al, you know? This was to be our fresh start."

He dropped his shovel and she walked to him. He touched his soiled fingers to the two frown marks recently etched in her brow. She linked her arms around him. His back was warm, damp.

When Pauline was outside picking shingle nails out of the grass, Alex got his carving knife from the pantry and descended into the cellar. He propped the flashlight on a shelf, aiming it at the barrel. He cut down into the salt. He speared a square piece of flesh and laid it on the stones. The edges were darkened yellow. He poked it with his knife. It was stiff but moist. He went upstairs, found some empty cartons in the attic and tiptoed back into the cellar with them. He cut pieces out of the salt and loaded them into the cartons. The barrel held mostly crusted salt which came out easily in chunks. These were put into the other cartons. He bailed out the remaining salt in his cupped hands. Six cartons crowded the stone floor.

He wiped his knife on his pants and his brow on his sleeve. He was sweating even in the cool.

He lifted one and carried it upstairs. On his way out the kitchen door he met Pauline with her bucket of nails.

"Oh," she said. "What's that?"

"Just some stuff."

"It's from the barrel, isn't it?"

"Yes. I've emptied the barrel."

She didn't look into the box. He edged through the door to the lawn and placed it on the grass. He walked past her, back into the cellar. When he carried up the second box she was in the kitchen rocker hugging her bucket, staring out the window. She stayed there as he carried the cartons up and out. The barrel was brought up last, heavy even when empty. He edged it up, step by step, and rolled it out to the cartons on the lawn. He loaded everything into the station wagon. Pauline came out with bags of trash. Alex added more from cleaning the barn. They drove to the town dump. They opened the back of the station wagon and heaved trash over the rim, sending rafts of seagulls squawking into the sky. They watched the cartons tumble down into garbage, broken glass, paper waste and mauled plastic bags. The barrel rolled down last, settling against a gutted washing machine. Alex found a rag in the car. "Want this?" She wiped her hands on it, threw it at the gulls, and it sailed away. — LN

On the bottom of the story Lee penned the word,

"Sentimental!" But she left it for me anyway. I find it otherwise.

The day before: Rich, a guy I used to play basketball with, past head of Black Studies at Dartmouth, where we'd graduated, calls me. He is now president of an "alternative" college in Vermont. His friend and our acquaintance, Bernie, is in trouble on Deer Island, and since Lee and I are in this area of Maine, Washington County, the most Downeast one can get, Rich asks if we'll go over— implying we might be respectable, as more or less local teachers (I do some substitution), and that he trusts us to see if we can make sense of things, help the rest of the students get home. Apparently, Bernie has been incoherent on the phone. He is always so articulate, too much so, in his ebullience. But Rick says he was incredibly rattled. Some might call Bernie charismatic, Ghanaian with an Oxford English accent. We know from Rick that one of Bernie's charges has hung herself. Lee says we'd better be careful. "I wish you didn't have a beard and long hair today." Bernie is delightful and so black, a Ghanaian prince…he lies, we think, with humor. His doctor parents were naturalized in the U.S. before he was born, but sent him from Queens to England to be educated.

We know Downeasters who have never met a "Black," even seen one on the street. We have to be careful, especially on an island that has sparse TV at best. Canadian Channel 4 comes in sometimes where we live. Lee can affect local, but she is elegant even in jeans and flannel shirt. For this trip she wears her steel-rimmed glasses, her hair pinned up in schoolmarm fashion. Her Kate Hepburn air. Though she looks more like Gene Tierney. I am wondering if we should tell the local authorities on Deer Island that Bernie is a Nam vet. It could be a good thing for some Canadians, but maybe bad for others, despite Bernie's charm. Many American kids have crossed into Canada to avoid the draft. I helped two. And found sympathy. Many Canadians can't understand why we went to Nam. Most of us don't really know either. Lee says, "Telling them about Bernie and Nam is too risky, not worth it, given the reception our guys back are getting. The rep for drugs." But I want to believe that Canadians are reasonable people, calmer than America's carnival nature can be. They have as many guns per capita as we do but a very low death by gun rate. Real gun laws, but I think it more a national tendency toward modesty. Maybe socialistic?

There is no one from the retreat to meet us, but Rich said Bernie had said to go southeast along the shore road and a few miles on we'd see yellow plastic police cordons tied to trees at a pale yellow Victorian farmhouse on the left. Lee is driving now and warns me to be polite, to listen and find out how to best help. She says, "Don't find something to argue about with anyone; don't identify some injustice. No hectoring." I say, "I think we are safe from my proclivities." I don't admire my self-righteousness, so easily agree when Lee says, "It's best I do the talking, see how the 'kids' are doing, see if they've contacted home." "OK," I say, "there's a phone in the farmhouse, because Bernie used it, and maybe the local police can help with communication. God, I hope Bangor or Ellsworth TV news people don't come; the ferry lands every three hours." Lee answers, "Not again until morning. I don't think this will make news. You imagine things. We'd better just establish ourselves favorably, right away, before it gets dark." Two-thirds of the group of sixteen on Bernie's retreat are women. We want all of them to remain quiet. We want no exposure for ourselves. We are already "not from heah." I will violate this caution.

I ask, "How about I talk with Bernie; we did a little bonding that time we visited Rich." That had been in Hanover, Bernie down from near Montpelier. Lee nodded. The "kids" were from the "alternative" college where Bernie was installed as an Aquarian guru, though he taught history and social psychology in brilliant fashion, getting students to read the difficult stuff. He lectured on civil disobedience and nonviolence, using Jesus and Gandhi but also Tolstoy and Melville and Joyce, often on the subject of human action as opposed to thought. Ishmael. Bernie was born in Ghana, a child in NYC, his mother naturalized when he was ten. He finished his PhD in Comp Lit at NYU on the GI Bill, is also gifted with spiritual bullshit, a great smile, delightful company. He has led the retreat to this rural and foreign seclusion where students can play instruments, talk Sufi or Buddhism, weave, paint and draw, make pots and raise some of their own greens for the summer. Bernie is ebony, unlike Rich, who is closer to Muhammad Ali's coffee with cream color.

We see the two Taurus police cars first, flashers off. An officer in blue lowers the yellow tape, writing down our Maine plate number on a small pad. He pats the winch; Lee drives in a bit and pulls off to the left on the lawn beneath a huge maple. The door of a police car further toward the house opens and a blazing red-jacketed Royal Canadian Mounted Police sergeant walks toward us. Lee stands tall. "Hello, I'm Lee Nilsen and this is my husband Tom. We are both teachers and have been asked to come see if the kids are OK and help arrange to get them back to school or parents." I see the officer appreciate Lee; he doesn't exactly smile, but nods, gentlemanly. "Good you've come. We are still investigating, so no one can leave the site. When that time comes, looks like soon, we'll get them ferried and have a bus take them through customs in Calais. The owners of this place"—he jerks his head back at the house—"Americans by the way, want a thorough inventory. They are sure their property value has plummeted. The place now jinxed. They want the apple tree cut down. I am Sergeant Dennis." He is as firm as his name. My typical resistance to, or envy of authority rises mildly in my craw. Are the police thinking beyond an unstable kid hanging herself? Despite the desire to control myself, I ask, "What about Sally?" I have to name her. Sergeant Dennis looks my way, patiently. "The body went over on the ferry, midday run, just after lunch. On the way to deliver her to the funeral home in Calais. Her parents made arrangements and are headed there. We did not think an autopsy was required. We took a blood sample. Routine." I nod, lower my eyes, say quietly, "Thank you." We may have passed the hearse or van on the way here, stateside. Sergeant Dennis says, "We just need to be sure how this happened. Why is interesting, but can't be recorded, so we are talking with each of the students." Lee nods to the Mountie: "Of course, I didn't mean to take the kids back right away, though the parents are anxious." Again, the Mountie nods. "You'd best go back to the studio where most of them have gathered for lunch. People brought food." Lee says, "That's wonderful." I wonder if island people are just curious, bring food as a way of getting a look. Then again, cynicism is the genius of the mediocre. Lee told me that one time. Somebody of note said it. The Mountie warns, "We've had young people from the States here to avoid your draft, over on the ferry or lobster boats, so we aren't exactly strangers. And we have some few American summer folk who own houses or rent here." We both nod. Things between Americans and these Canadians are self-conscious now, if they ever weren't.

Just before I met Lee, I helped arrange for two boys coming up on draft age, the sons of college teachers from Connecticut, to sneak over and seek asylum, crossing at Calais to St. Stephen on the St. Croix River. All this crossing water. What happened to those boys? I took them across ostensibly to go figure skating, where they were picked up afterward by other dodgers, one a relative. It was a neat ploy, people from Downeast crossing to skate or see hockey games at the Border Arena. Lee and I have skated there at least once a week in season, Lee teaching me my edges and figures and then sweeping off across the ice doing quick inside and outside three-turns, a Mohawk or two before settling on a hockey circle to do fine figure eights. I am almost clumsy. After skating and delivering the kids to their intermediary contact, a local expat and assistant hockey coach in St. Andrews, I recrossed at the Milltown Gate a mile or so upriver from the Calais crossing. No questions, my skates glinting on the seat beside me. They did not notice that three crossed and one returned.

I want to see Bernie, so excuse myself and leave Lee to go to the studio because I see another Mountie go into the back door of the house with Bernie. He is slumped in a kitchen chair, his hand around a coffee mug. "How you doin'?" Bernie looks up. "Tom! I am so glad to see you.

This is the worst day of my life." A pause, and then he says, "I really thought I was on top of things here. It is an existential nightmare. Hell, she did it in an apple tree!" Bernie's quick way of moving the real into academic perspective with this allusion pisses me off. "You mean Sally? What happened?"

Bernie doesn't seem to mind that the Mountie is near enough to hear, but where to be private, anyway? Conscience? Or just a black man running from hounds. Sidney Poitier. Now I'm doing it, looking for distraction. The Mountie is making more coffee on the old Glenwood, stoking it with alder sticks. Bernie says, "I have already told the RCMP all I know. Do I have to repeat it to you?" He is pissed. "Only if you think I should know," I answer. "Oh, well, I guess . . . her name is, was, Sally Klein, from Brooklyn. Not much confidence but sexually aggressive." The Mountie looks around at Bernie. I interrupt. "Bernie, did you say that to the RCMP right away?" "No, just about her confidence." The Mountie looks back at the stove. Bernie is panicking. "I mean she can't stand to be rejected about anything. Couldn't stand, I mean. She cooked the night before and drove us all crazy about whether we liked the food. It was OK, lentils and beans and onions with cumin and tomato sauce, but she wouldn't let it go until she finally started crying, saying she couldn't do anything right. One other kid, one I know slept with her, said, 'Not true . . . you have a great singing voice.' That helped some. But Sally showed no suicidal intent, not since last year on campus when she threatened, verbally. Not unusual on campuses. Was she thinking of some kind of ritual last supper she had cooked?" I am still pissed at Bernie's intellectualizing. The way Lee gets with me. She may be the real intellectual. Then Bernie says, "I talked to the parents, who called after the RCMP informed them. I was OK, cool enough for them. They seemed almost relieved... no, that's not right... calm, as if sad and stunned by the inevitable? I don't know. I just don't know. You know?" Now I feel like a self-righteous jerk. I wonder why we need to think we should know. The Mountie has heard every word without reaction.

I don't say to Bernie, or Lee, that maybe Sally wasn't right for this kind of venture, this kind of theater. Bernie will really clam up if I indict his choices. His is a very liberal school. I know that our invasion of Vietnam took him across hostile borders. That he killed no one, worked logistics and entertainment. But still felt guilty. Bernie is drama prone. He is if anything guilty of overwhelming sincerity. Years later, the elder philosopher from Princeton, Frankfurt, will write a slim book concluding that "sincerity itself is bullshit." A favorite fortune cookie. The Mountie takes his coffee and a full cup for Sergeant Dennis out into the yard, toward the cars. I look hard at Bernie for a bit, decide and ask, "Did you sleep with her?" Bernie looks surprised but finally says, "Yes. Does that have to come out?" "When was that?" Bernie shakes his head as if he can't remember . . . "Two nights after we got here, two weeks ago." He lowers his voice and leans toward me. "We were all pretty stoned." I ask, "Has Sergeant Dennis asked? Do they know about the pot smoking?" "Not for sure, Tom, but they act like they are sure of everything." "Don't get paranoid, Bernie. We need to stay clear here." I am taking my lead from Lee's urgent common sense.

I take an apple off the table and go outdoors, hoping the Mounties just want to be quit of us all. Lee is in a group of students on the lawn. A couple of the girls are talking. One, a small blond in white bib overalls covered with paint and clay, says, "She didn't let on, just sulked a lot. The stepmother sent her off to camps, boarding schools. Said she'd been thrown out of the last camp for an affair with the senior camp counselor, a guy her father's age. Her stepmother kept arranging to get her out of the house, bribing her with trips, shopping, stuff like that. She actually took up shoplifting to get her real mother's attention. That's what her therapist told her. Her real mother lives in California and wouldn't have her there, though they talked once in a while on the phone. Her 'unnatural mother' she called her. She said she also wanted to go away to schools or camps to get away from the stepmother. She was obsessive about that. But you don't go and kill yourself over stuff like this, do you? I mean, my parents are divorced. I mean she never had anything going with her real mother. Probably doesn't even know her kid has offed herself." The blond is beginning to get into it. So Lee says, "You know, even psychiatrists can't get to what is more than basic beneath the symptoms of mental disorder. They have to be prepared to give up on standard scenarios. And it won't do us any good to speculate unless you remember Sally saying something specific about killing herself while she was here. Probably her parents and the shrink she saw will be able to put up a fair picture over time. As part of their own therapy. Do any of you think you had a role in what happened?"

This is a brilliant question, not accusative, Lee's tone rendering silence, even consideration. Lee is so damned smart. But no one offers anything. Her question leaves them adult. I think to seek out the kid who slept with her and see if he has any ideas. He is sitting in front of Lee with a blank look on his face. He could be conscience stricken, or gone feral. Bernie would have told me (or would he?) if he thought he or the kid had precipitated the suicide. He said they were just stoned when they "played" with each other.

When I tell Lee that hers was a brilliant question, she says, "I never should have asked it. Let the police handle it; don't interfere." "Yeah," I say, "and I won't go after the boy she was sleeping with." Lee nods, "Let's go find some lunch. I don't think there is a restaurant this side of the island. We can make something from what's in the studio. Cold potato salad there. We don't want to be noticed by anyone beyond here anyway."

Later, wanting to fix things fast, I come up with an idea and ask if they all feel like some exercise, a walk down the wood road across from the house to the bay. A change of scene. They seem OK about that. I walk out to the cars where the Mounties are sitting, Sergeant Dennis hanging up his dispatch phone. "Hi, would it be OK if we took the kids for a walk down the wood road to the bay? Tomorrow morning? It might be good for them to exercise. I don't think many of them know how to think about this and may want to ask dumb questions away from here." The Mounties look at each other and Sergeant Dennis says, "OK, the same people who own this house own that land down to the cove . . . but keep together, quietly . . . no singing or antic behavior. People here watch strangers. And I'd appreciate knowing if you learn anything we haven't. I don't like assumptions. We are going back to Headquarters; you have our phone." I answer, "OK, the walk will be no problem. The kids are too subdued." He replies, "You never know when people are excited." He walks away. Lee seethes, "I wish you'd asked me about this. It is not a good idea to do anything but get the hell off this island. Don't you know enough from home about how local people react to disturbances to their sense of things? These kids don't belong here, never did.

We are not taking this walk!"

"Look," I say, "we aren't going to make a mess of things. A walk is normal. We need normal." I am getting defensive. Lee asks, "If one of them were your kid would you leave these grounds? Under these conditions?" I do pause, but not long enough: "These are the same people as home, so how come you want a child among them?" It comes out like that. Lee turns and walks back to the Travelall, sits on the tailgate. I walk over and say, "Let's take the damn walk and go home, OK?" Lee, without looking at me, says, "OK." It doesn't register that she is about done with me. I rationalize the walk as a good thing to protect my idea, my plan, my control. My movie. I haven't asked Lee.

We are anxious to get the kids on their way and get back to Vito. Once it's dark, the kids don't feel like talking anymore and move away from each other to read, sleep, sit on the back porch. We don't smell any pot. We drop the tailgate on the Travelall and crawl in on the mattress after brushing aside some dog hair. Lee digs in the big duffle and hauls out the quilt, in case the sleeping bag isn't warm enough. It gets chilly on the island, summer nights. We strip to our underwear and crawl in. Lee says nothing. Ashamed of my instincts at a time like this, I am silent. Lee says, "I want to talk with Vito about all this, about everything." I don't register any threat, just her discomfort.

After breakfast we start down the wood road to the

bay. Lee says, "It is good that we are all dispirited." Sort of wandering along, I think. She tells the legend that the pirate Morgan is said to have hidden treasure in a cave at the cove we are approaching. The one obese boy with us asks if the place has been searched by professors, because metal detectors won't pick up gold. Lee recounts that searches have been made since the early 1800s. There are two caves with markings by various visitors for well over a century at least. "So we won't find anything either, right," says the fat kid. "I don't think so," says Lee, "but maybe that's not why to go there. Maybe it's just to be quiet in a place that has such history, such ghosts." "There are no ghosts," says the kid. "No," says Lee. "But I like to imagine what people looked like who have been here so long ago. What they wore. Maybe even some of my relatives. And Indians long before who weren't interested in gold, but maybe nails, needles and mirrors once we came. Screened artifacts from the clamshell banks all around here and Maine have been carbon dated to 1900 B.C." The small blond asks, "Did they kill seals?" Lee says, "I don't know, but probably. Maybe the cove was for shelter, a place for a fire and rest after digging clams or spearing lobster and flounder in the shallows." I say, "I am sure they ate seals. All indigenous coastal people did, and cured the skins. How many people do you think the caves could sleep?" We bend a little and step only a few feet into the first cave; its floor runs to rock wall maybe thirty feet back. People have had fires inside recently, given the fire pit and melted beer bottles and aluminum cans. "Artifacts," I say. No one laughs. They wander, scuffing at gravel, acting now like grade school kids. I reflect again on Lee's genius as a teacher, going from such a simple question into talking about anthropological questions, like were the Algonquins here only in summer, or did a few stay on through winter, if any. She explains how winter, when Indians could move in snow and over the ice on lakes, was the big hunting time for getting meat and furs, that summers were for bonding with families and other tribal groups, living easy off shellfish, fish, berries, and dried meat. We try then to imagine what ceremonies might have been. Beyond the stereotypes we have from movies. What do people dance for? Did anyone dance for themselves within the ritual, if that is what it was. There is talk about rock concerts, conformity, dress. The bay opens before us as we turn from the two caves under the trees and walk down on the gravel and jasper beach to the incoming tide. Some take off their shoes and wade in the painful then numbing cold. Penance, I think, because they do not giggle or squeal. Just grimace. They sit on rocks and eat their sandwiches, peanut butter and jelly. Kids. But the boy Sally slept with asks, "Did Indians ever commit suicide?"

I wait for someone to bring up Sally, but it is as if there is nothing to say, no self-incriminations, no secret knowledge. No discussion of the question about Indians. So we start back. I think everyone is very tired of Deer Island. And I have read that Morgan's treasure legend is about Deer Island, Maryland, though I don't say so. The farmhouse seems to have reclaimed itself. The afternoon passes in silence, no chatter, no music. The walk seems a good thing. I think about Vito as I fall asleep with little sense of Lee lying beside me or knowing if she can sleep. I can't ask.

Sergeant Dennis joins us for coffee in the morning. Relieving the silence. "Well," he says, "the higher-ups are ready for you to leave. I called American customs and they won't ask for more than IDs but will xerox each, make sure everyone is back. I took the liberty of explaining Ernie's accent and background, that he is an American citizen under no suspicion. And a Vietnam veteran. That should smooth things. No one wants to make a big thing out of this girl's tragedy. The ferry will leave at fourteen-hundred hours this afternoon, so you'd best get them packing." Lee stands and takes his hand, saying, "We could not have hoped for better care than you have taken; we know how hard it is for islanders to have this happen on their island. We live on a dirt road. It is very quiet." The Sergeant nods, gives me an acknowledging glance and walks off. An island school bus shows up to take the for once efficient students to the ferry landing. It is a gloomy day on the bay, but we can see some sunlight beneath the clouds to the west as we steer back to America.

I am thinking that I could live on Deer Island. Why I cannot say, but say so to Lee, just to stay in touch. She answers, "Tom, you are too young to want anything over with." I do not like this objectivity. But indulge it on my own. A girl is dead. Probably cremated by now. People getting on with their grief and "self-conscious lives." The chorus' catharsis, urge to return to normal. I want that, but "normal" seems remote just now.

Driving back to the farm, sixteen miles from customs in Calais, Lee says matter of factly, "I'm jealous. Did I tell you Kim is pregnant and wants to get married? Makes sense!" I say, "So that's what we should have done," before I can think about how this might pinch. Lee says, "We had a great time before getting married and never talked about children. I just wanted your body." "Yeah," I say, "and all I wanted was your mind." She slides over on the bench seat and drops her head on my shoulder, dozes until fried clams on Route 1 in Robbinston. Am I thinking everything is OK now?

The farmyard is dark when we pull in, no lamps casting pee-colored stains on the lawn. We have stopped to pick up Toby from Sam, who is up for the gossip, but Lee easily says, "Maybe in a few days, OK? It was hard." Sam says, "Don't forget his bowl and food." He returns inside to his TV shows on his black and white Zenith.

It is a very fast and separate night. Toby between us. At dawn, I walk back to the pasture with Toby and count the sheep. The beef critter, a Holstein steer, stands stupid by the gate, so I give him a fallen apple. The steer crunches it and slobbers. I am walking back when I hear a car on the road, a car door slam. It has to be Vito. I trot to the kitchen, find Lee just pulling out of Vito's hug. Toby bumps his thighs, tunnels between his legs. A Rottweiler trait, when they like someone. She has said that Vito is the most beautiful man she has ever laid eyes on, "a cross between Vittorio Gassman and Gregory Peck." I knew Gassman from the movie *Bitter Rice*, with Silvana Mangano. This is Vito's third summer visit and we say to him that we need him around while events on the island digest, but regret involving him. Vito nods. We get him settled in his room, which means I take up his one bag and Lee checks the wick in his bedside oil lamp. When he comes back down he brings foil-wrapped lasagna from Tony's on Federal Hill in Providence. Vito says, "Farm people eat big at 11 a.m." I go to the barn and bring in a pitcher of cold homebrew. We talk about long drives, his and ours. An osprey over water at Wiscasset. No deer. No moose. Few Winnebagos. That afternoon we walk without talking much along the gravel beach at May's Cove. That evening, some smoked ham sandwiches on Lee's leftover ciabatta and two bottles of Vito's wine. We are all still tired and go to blessed sleep. Toby snoring, levitating.

On the morning tide I walk down to the skiff, row out to my small lobster boat, start the engine and putt down the bay a half mile to my string of five traps. I do not rebait the crates after removing the eight lobsters, but stack them forward and on top of the cuddy. It is near the end of the season onshore, though the commercial guys will fish further out for at least another month, maybe until December. After that they'll gear up their scallop drags. Lee is baking sourdough. The kind with yeasty, almost translucent elasticity and holes that pool butter. And there is still tender salad in the shadier rows nearest the barn. Broccolini to sauté. Vito brings in the whole case of his family's wine from the trunk of the clerically black Volvo, puts it down in the root cellar to perfectly cool. Sam is invited, much to Toby's delight, so Lee has her kitchen full of men, all four in love with her. The wine is pure Tuscan, discreetly dry, some fruit, earth tones, a touch of tobacco in the finish. I say this and Lee says, "It's just a delicious wine, dammit." Sam drinks homebrew because, as he says, "Wine is for wops and spics. Garlic, too," recalling the air in the old theater in Bristol, full of Italians and Portuguese. "All they drank was wine, not American, right in the theater, out of the bottle." Vito takes this with good humor, reminds Sam he is an Italian. Sam says, "I don't mean you, but these two don't know no better, not when there's good beer." Sam likes this ale I make, triple hopped, from New Zealand malt. Vito says he loves my ale when he is thirsty, but otherwise it is "vino." Sam is not "into" sipping, so right after he downs his lobster, bread, salad, and ice cream with Lee's chocolate sauce laced with brandy, he trundles off lopsided down the hill as if the yacht were heeling. He has his programs to watch. Saturday nights, *The Honeymooners,* followed by Lawrence Welk. Sam has a crush on "Little Anna Kane," Welk's token Latina, a very modest version of Xavier Cugat's "Chica Chica Boom Chic." Sam goes into spasms laughing at Ed Norton, the sewer worker.

I look at Vito and Lee and feel it is an OK time, so I say, "You know, Vito, we just can't find anything to say or think; a girl hung herself in a tree. Bernie, you've heard me mention him, the Ghanaian guy, blames himself, not for having slept with her but because he was in charge and his charisma failed." Lee says, "That's a hard appraisal, but probably fair. It's just that no one seems to have known Sally except as a bunch of superficial symptoms. More than one of the kids is probably depressed, though not clinically diagnosed. Sally came to school with no records. It's that sort of school. Idealists covering for Yankee pragmatism. Dewey-ites. Maybe the parents wanted to hide them, can pay the bill." Vito shakes his head slowly. "Even God doesn't know what is going on, sometimes," he says, "if He did he couldn't stay interested." He smiles. We know he is thinking while he speaks. I say, "That just wouldn't really be God, not the one so many talk to.

Grounds for me to join the faith. Except no one listens to my talk." Vito laughs, "Maybe someday. Remember, I did not go into the church as a deep believer. I became a priest in mild detachment from this world." Am I like this, too? I say, "You'd get along with Camus, though he didn't have a second life to go to." Vito takes a long sip, smiles at the wine glass and refills it. "You know, the idea of heaven is so old, and it has helped so many to, how you say, 'deal.'" "Yes," I say, "but so many faithful give up on this world, don't care about the animals, the rivers, the other races. It's like they have a way out. At least Camus leaves us with full responsibility." Lee begins to clear dishes. She knows this isn't going anywhere. "True, but there are many who care, do good work even while depressed or in bad health because they feel some gentle possibility after hard life. It is OK. In a way we all remain responsible for this life, whether we are selfish or not. God cannot know because that would be cheating." He laughs. But I wonder if anyone can be this benign, and if there is another layer to his thinking that can never come out. Maybe I am just hubristic. Men fear exposure, I think again.

Lee knows my habit of working off a hangover by staying up, filling the two wash basins with hot and rinse water, turning on the battery-operated Panasonic land radio that quietly brings in the late night Chicago jazz station, WBGO. In the morning the kitchen will be clean, dishes stacked and dry, silverware filed, knives dried and placed in their slots by the bread board. She says, "Well, I've had my two glasses and I'm woozy, also still pretty beat. Goodnight you two, I love you." She walks out of the kitchen, both of us knowing loss. "Vito, I never know what she is really thinking." "That is the way with such a woman," he says. How could he know? Toby pads behind Lee to bed.

Next morning before breakfast, before Vito is up, I take the tractor down to the shore and haul the trailer and boat, lobster crates still tied down on top, up into the field. I unhitch the trailer and hitch up the small paneled cart made from a pickup bed to the tractor, then load the crates in that, along with the boat's mooring line and buoys. I will come down later for the skiff, which I have pulled up on the gravel and tied up to alders. I back the cart into the barn, unhitch and park the tractor. In the kitchen I find Vito and Lee over coffee. The granola is untouched, so they have waited for me. I pour coffee and feel awkward. They have been talking about me, or "us," and I am downed by my fear that our marriage has been taken to the table like a damaged child, to be discussed empathetically, clinically. I feel self-conscious. But I have absolutely nothing to say and talk goes to normal: "Who wants apples cut on the granola. Anyone for an egg and bread, fried? More coffee? Do you have enough, Tom, for a second cup? We're on thirds." So breakfast continues and we plan a walk to the cove again at the other end of the peninsula, where we wear boots and wade around the rocks at low tide, picking mussels. Then we will argue, as we scrape off the barnacles and "beards," about how we will cook them. Bathed in white wine, butter and rosemary? Butter and garlic? Baked in our canned tomato sauce with a dust of parmesan? Or white wine and pesto? We do this while sipping Vito's wine in the battered wooden lawn chairs. Toby snuffles the barnacles and beards and gives up. Talk turns to island life, rural life, how its intensity differs from, say, Hartford. The parish. What happens to children there, or here, with both parents working low wage jobs that still don't hold off debt. I know a lobsterman whose boat loans from the FHA run to more than a quarter million. After payments, cost of traps, gas, insurance, permits and taxes he nets about $25,000 a year, not enough for much of a house or truck or getting a kid through college. Yet he has a damaged lumbar at age thirty-eight from the sheer labor of his work. Vito says how there are those who think such people need to pick themselves up by their bootstraps and make more money. His parish now has some Somalis to join the blacks and Latinos whose jobs include cleaning rooms, toilets, and showers and making beds for area hotel chains. Work at car washes, city garbage removal, bridge painting and filling potholes. Lee says she tried once to make a bed as tight as a hotel guest expects, and failed. That it is very hard on the knees and back and shoulders. Vito says, "I do not make my bed. God did not make my bed, so I do not." He is serious. Lee says, lightly, "You mean you can't get a friendly nun to come in once a day?" Vito laughs loudly, says, "I have not found one that *perfetto*."

Mussels cleaned, for classic sauvignon blanc, butter and garlic, decision made: we drive to the lake and bathe with Ivory soap at the boat landing. Toby swims around, brings a tossed stick back, but he is a half-hearted retriever, would rather just swim around and then shake all over us. We hang our bathing suits on the line and I think the four of us are happy enough. We plan ahead for our next visit with each other. Lee has introduced Vito to Kim and her "after the fact" fiancé, her guy.

Kim also went to Wellesley and also did things her way. It is quite a wedding. Getting out of the car, Lee and I hear a bagpipe wailing in the fog, out on the lawn beyond the broad veranda that wraps the gray, cedar-shingled Victorian hotel settled on its granite perch. The water is not visible but we smell the salt tang and the iodine, perfect with the groan and whine of the heart-rending music. I love being slightly chilled and hope to get a little drunk, for a wedding of people I don't know but whose spirits show in choosing such a fantastical site. A bagpipe beats an organ anytime, and visibility should be low at any wedding. Nobody knows what they are doing when they get married. That's the point of it. No clear hopes, plans or apprehensions. Lust is fine. The fog.

Lee talks to the gravid but cheerful bride. We have given up on Dr. Duffy. Our sex life has been OK. I chalk this up to what happens in marriage. We are considerate, generous, not wild. Needy. I am aware that we do not talk anymore about having children. Maybe we just want to let whatever happens happen. But it is too easy to assume that Lee doesn't much care anymore.

Back along the long polished cherrywood bar in the hotel I fall to talking with Vito, who has arrived, invited because Kim knows Lee and Vito are close and because he will be staying with us. Lee wants Vito to know Kim. I say that I like having the wedding here, "sort of pagan and funky." I mean no challenge. Vito agrees, says a wedding is a pagan sacrament as well. The old hotel is unusual for a wedding, as is the music of the bagpipe under the huge, quiet spruce. The fog dragging on the Victorian spires. It is a civil wedding, despite the groom's parents' Anglican leanings. Vito says, "It is a time in America and in Italy of independence of the young from culture. From history. Though maybe it has always been so." I think of the pendulum swinging, disaster waiting. He lifts his glass of wine and says, "A toast to the young." Though he and I are only in our early thirties. I say, "You are one pragmatic priest, Father Vito." "And you are a would-be dreamer, and I am Vito, not your father." He laughs. "I'm just Tom; I try." "You prove my point," says

Vito. We lift our single malts, delighted.

The wedding ceremony is a brief pleasure and the band of teenagers from Belfast gets everyone dancing except Vito and me. And the bagpiper who stands at the other end of the bar drinking and talking with the bartender. He is tall, maybe twenty, long blond hair tied back with a ribbon Celtic style, tartan kilt and hard black shoes, the kind clog-dancers wear. Lee is a great dancer and she finds one partner after another in what is an everyone dances with everyone else affair, the bride lifting her wedding dress to show her bright white sneakers with pink laces. Lee can boogie or Charleston or twist or country chicken step, or anything else. Swings her hips, hula style.

Vito follows us back up Route 1 to the farm. We arrive in full moonlight, do not have to cook because we stopped for clams in Millbridge. At the Red Barn. For the occasion I have bought Rémy Martin, so we have some at the kitchen table without a lamp, the moon so bright the pepper shaker casts a shadow like a little man. The short lawn outside looks as if it has been dusted with a light snow. Sam has relinquished Toby, snoozing at our feet. Vito says, "Before I do ablutions and go to bed, there is something I want to tell you." My mind alerts a bit. "You remember the bagpipe player?" I say, "Yeah, he is going to marine architecture school at the university in Dalhousie." "Well," says Vito, "he is interning with an architect in Belfast now, so you may see him when you visit Kim and John. His name is Dell and he and John ran together at summer sailing camp." "Good," I say, "I'll keep him in mind." Lee says, "I tried to get him to dance; he seemed somber as his music. Great legs in that kilt. You guys talk; I'm off to bed." She signals Toby, who now sleeps with his head on Lee's legs. She loves him there. I have trained him with my big toe to avoid my knees, which ache some, every night. "So what's up with the bagpiper, er, Dell . . . ?" I hear Lee close the bedroom door and I pour us another finger of cognac. "You remember the events on Deer Island?" "Of course," I say, "What's up? Did the bagpiper know of it?" "Yes, he did." "Newspaper? TV? Must have come from TV in Bangor." "No, Dell was there. He grew up on the island." "No shit," I say, " . . . so what did he think?" "It was not what he thought, but what he did." "O God, come on, Vito . . ." "Tom, the time you took the students on a walk down to the bay? Well, Dell and his uncle, a drinker, followed you along the ridge above the road in the woods." "Spying, I guess," I said. "The Mountie sergeant told me that locals would be suspicious. Lee didn't want to take the walk, afraid of them, or something." Vito sips, swirls the cognac. "Tom, Dell had a deer rifle and held crosshairs on your head." Then Vito pushes his chair back as a way of giving me time to settle and think. "Oh Jesus," I say.

Vito manages a laugh, says, "Strange how non-theists

come around, how do you say, 'in a pinch.'" I am more than pinched. I see a flash of bright hair blasted with brain and blood and bone shards. I have hunted enough, killed sheep with a pistol as well, for fall butchering. I have a pretty exquisite sense of what a high-powered rifle projectile can do. For seconds I am totally selfish, imagining. It is more powerful than the image of the eel clamping on my thumb, by far. But it does not hurt; it is already fantasia; my ego is insulted. I am avoiding the implications. For a split second I see the bagpiper jigging with Lee in garish Technicolor, mocking me, because I am not real after all. I am a fraud. And Lee knows it.

Vito speaks. "Tom, it was a sincere confession; he was disturbed, just seeing you at the wedding. A Catholic. Upset at how close he'd come to that violence. I can understand how a young man can get caught up in local enthusiasms." "Enthusiasms," that is Vito's word. How much humor a priest must have to stay sane.

A year after Lee moved out, Vito sent me another story Lee had written and given to him. His note said: "Tom, *mio amico*, I am passing this on to you. Lee gave it to me to try to understand why she loved but gave up. Please keep in touch. — Vito"

GETTING BY

Gail woke. Something was moving in her garden. She knew; it was the steer again. "Hon, wake up. The cow's out." She groped from the bed for her shirt and shorts on top of the bureau. Bill droned, "Where this time?" He shoved his pillow, opened one eye, squinted. "Where?" "My lettuce." He pushed back the covers, sat up among crumpled blankets. The black and white beast was tearing mouthfuls of Gail's October lettuce.

She tugged at sleeves, buttons. "Hurry up."

He pried himself out of bed. "OK, OK." He bumped out the screen door into a bright morning while zipping his pants. She was already on the barn ramp swiping at mosquitoes. He slid the door open and jerked a coil of rope off its hook. Gail tilted the top from the grain barrel, filled a coffee can, and poured grain into a pan. They crossed between the barn and house to the massive culprit in her garden. Bill approached with the rope.

"No, dammit! He's scared of rope. Let me try grain."

He shrugged, closed his arms across his chest. The steer was idly munching and looked up. Strands of oakleaf lettuce festooned his mouth. He blinked dumb black eyes with sly cunning, willing to challenge forbidden territory. He nosed Gail's pan aside and chomped the oakleaf. Bill watched.

"No go. I'll try apples." She ran back to the barn and grabbed a five-gallon plastic bucket. She ran to the nearest apple tree and shook its lowest branch. Apples tumbled to the ground. She threw them in the bucket so that the simple creature would hear his favorite food. He suspended chewing and watched. Gail tossed an apple near him. "Come on, you castrated creep, you ball-less bastard. Apples make your juicy steaks."

He took a step and ate the apple. She threw another. He ate it. Bill shifted behind with the rope over his arm. The beast gathered momentum, lumbering toward Gail as she paced backwards, tossing a trail of apples on the path to the pasture.

When she got to the gate she laid an apple line in offering, and as he slobbered and crunched them she lifted the latch. With measured slowness she opened the gate. She trailed more apples inside, he followed, and Bill swung the gate shut.

"Not much fence left. Almost all patches now." He tweaked a limp wire strand that was hooked in his cuff.

"Look at you. Bare feet in your good shoes."

"Honey, I am doing the very best I can with what little we've got." He swatted the rope at a manure bun on his shoetop. "The damn thing will break out again if I don't fix the hole. Soon." Bill went back up the path.

She hurried to catch up. She offered her empty bucket and he flipped the rope into it. She summoned meager cheer. "Next time let's buy one who's trained to a rope. I bet we're the only people in Maine with a wild cow."

Bill gathered barbed wire, nails and cutters, picked up his work gloves, and saw somebody running down the road. A lanky young man in jacket and tie was chasing a black dog, which veered off into the field across the road. The man saw the two people and swerved into their dooryard. His eyes were anguished.

"My cousin's being buried up in the graveyard," he waved his arm up toward the rooftops of a line of cars, "and this goddamn dog is running around. Do you have a rope or something?"

"Sure, let's catch it." Bill took his rope from the bucket and hurried toward the young man.

"Wait a minute." Gail raised her hand to delay them. "Use bait. It works." She went in the kitchen door and returned with a hunk of hamburger. Bill was pulling the rope as if to stretch it. He threw it down, tore at the meat and passed half to the young man. The dog was panting and watching. They approached from each side, offering meat at arm's length. Bill tossed his toward the dog as Gail had done with the steer.

"Whose funeral?" he asked.

"Bob Tate. John Tate's his father."

"John Tate who owns blueberry land?"

"That's him."

They had seen John only once, when an airplane spraying pesticide on John's blueberries had banked over their own land and spray drifted into their pasture. Gail had moaned, "All our work at organic farming, he has no right to do this to us." So they went to John's house. His wife had sat the whole time grim and silent at the kitchen table. John was in an easy chair with his hands on his knees. Through his tobacco chaw he'd said, "It's the business of the pilot and the spray company, not mine. It's no threat to human or animal anyway. I been growing blueberries all my life."

The dog did not take the bait. He sulked farther away.

Bill said, "You'd better get back to the funeral. I'll watch and chase him off."

The young man tossed his hamburger into the weeds. He ran back up the road, his necktie flapping.

Gail was squatting in her garden, trying to tuck the carrots into their rows and to stuff uprooted lettuce back into the soil.

She saw Bill pulling on his workgloves. "Hon, we have to talk about the cow. He's costing us over a dollar a day."

"We have no choice. It's been too dry."

"I haven't got much garden stuff left. We can't keep him in and we're getting more behind every day." Her arm waved at the apple trees in a salute of despair. "Frost is getting the apples, and that's the only free food around. May as well buy our meat at the store."

"It's still too warm. How many times must I tell you, you can't hang beef in warm weather? Too many flies. It'll load with maggots and go bad. We've got to wait. And if it doesn't hang, what? We'll get tough meat. Two hundred fifty pounds of tough, green meat, that's what."

"Yeah, I know. I really do. I just get so frustrated. Boy, sitting behind a desk was so simple compared to this."

"And boring, my dear? Do you remember just how boring?"

"A crashing bore." She handed him a limp pile of lettuce.

Bill jammed it into the compost. "We're doing OK. In just six months we've gotten a lot done here. As long as we can keep part-time work, we'll be OK. I believe we'll be OK. Trust me, please?"

He was just turning toward the pasture with his tools and wire when he heard the shot. It came from the graveyard. Gail rose up from her lettuce. "The dog?"

He dropped his equipment. Both ran across the lawn and up the road. The cars were gone except for one pickup truck with lights across the top. They saw a man. They saw a black and white hump near him. John Tate, in a black suit and white shirt, stood cradling a gun. His tie was loosened and his glasses were askew. The steer lay quivering on the ground with blood oozing from his head. John Tate looked at the two young people coming toward him. Grief and anger twisted his sweaty face. Fresh dirt was scattered all around him. A hollow gaped below his feet. Nearby gravestones were splattered with blood. Crushed and mangled ribbons and flower baskets laced the grass. The steer had dirt halfway up his legs, and bits of pink and yellow petals were wedged in his hooves. Soil clots, flowers, stems and ferns were strewn everywhere.

"He walked on that grave." John's voice was flat. "He walked on his grave." John turned away from Gail, Bill and the dead steer and walked with his gun to the truck. Without glancing back toward the three figures among the gravestones, he rolled his truck down the driveway and was gone.

The dirty bloody beast lay before them.

"What'll we do?" Gail implored the relentless brilliance of the sky.

"We cut. Now. Fast." Bill ran back to the house and Gail jogged to keep up.

He opened the van. Boxes, lumber, wire and bundles were cluttered inside. "Your goddam breads." Bill reached for a carton. "Get your breads out of here!"

She raced to rescue the cartons. "My breads make us some money just in case you care."

"I need space. Room to pack."

"I never complained about your stupid vacuum cleaners in here." She hauled the second box and put it with the first on the lawn.

Bill shoved out the other contents and swiftly packed his chainsaw, two sawhorses and three planks, his largest knife, and a meatsaw. Gail came from the woodshed carrying two washtubs, some large sheets of plastic, and her only roll of paper towels. Bill slammed the door; they drove up the gravel road to the graveyard. He drew the van close to the steer without leaving the cemetery path. He suddenly had no desire to violate anybody else's plot. Then he opened the van and they carried its contents to the carcass lying on the ground. Flies were already swarming its face. Bill set up sawhorses beside the lifeless hulk. He set the three planks across them. Gail lined up her washtubs. She wasn't sure what they'd be used for but they looked necessary to whatever business was about to be accomplished.

She scuffed bloodsoaked grass around the head and flies buzzed off. "I hope nobody comes to lay flowers."

"There's going to be more mess than this." Bill faced the steer with his knife. "Better take a walk, OK?"

Gail strolled among the headstones, trying to study the names of the dead. The chainsaw roared and coughed where Bill was moving quickly behind his makeshift table. The view from the graveyard, a postcard of autumn hills ignited with color, was ravaged by Bill's frantic activity. She was sitting at the lower end when she heard him call. She dodged headstones, ready to turn her head to save her stomach. Bill's shirt was on the ground and he stood in his Save the Trees T-shirt soaked with a frenzy of blood marks. His beard glistened with shreds of fat. His arms were red up to the elbows. The animal's head on the ground stared with one astonished eye at the heap of slimy grey, green stomachs and intestines sealed with Bill's bloody fingerprints. The black and white hide lay crumpled like an old coat discarded in the October sun. Four severed legs and cloven hooves with crushed flower petals inside were cast off, as if they were ready for reassembling.

Bill started his chainsaw and ran it down the backbone. Grass, gristle and bits of flowers spewed off the blade and the carcass fell into halves. Gail was amazed at how large the stomach cavity was once the guts were gone. You could crawl in there and lie down.

"Oh God. Gail. I hear a car." Bill froze with the chainsaw in one hand, his Save the Trees T-shirt now unintelligible with blood. A truck pulled into the graveyard. It was John Tate's. "Oh God, oh God."

John got out, closed the door and went to the bed of his truck. His black suit was rumpled and black tie was gone, and his white shirt was open at the throat. Gail faced him, trying to block the grisly evidence. John was carrying a hoe, a rake and a shovel. As he walked briskly toward them he appeared not to see the carnage. He put down his rake and hoe, and slowly began to scoop dirt back into the grave pit with the shovel.

Gail walked over to the hoe and picked it up. She moved beside John to level off the dirt that he transported back to the grave. Bill turned and tried to resume his butchering with a minimum of motion and noise, hoping he might become invisible. The steer was now two bloody halves. Bill bent to lift one half up onto the planks but between its weight and slippery surface he couldn't get any grip. He tried again. He tried to drag it. The half was too heavy. John put down his shovel and walked over to Bill. He leaned and got a grip at the other end of the side. Bill grabbed his end and together they hoisted it up onto the planks.

"Thanks," Bill whispered, as if with a louder voice John's son might rise up out of the hole.

"You better halve that side before you try to heft it again," John said.

Bill picked up his chainsaw.

John looked at the half. "Cuts cleaner with a knife."

"How do I get through the bones?"

"Here." John pointed to a spot between two verte-brae. "Cut here."

Bill tried. It wouldn't cut. The knife was stuck upright in the backbone. John reached for it and Bill loosened his grip. John wrenched it out and moved it a little lower. He bore down heavily and the side parted, rocking into two portions, fore and hind, and they suddenly looked like pieces of beef instead of a dead steer. John and Bill lowered the ends onto plastic sheets and lifted them into the van.

Gail began collecting bits of fat and bone that littered the ground, separating trampled flowers from the rest. She put the waste in the washtubs and the flowers in a neat pile near the grave. The men lifted the other side to the planks, slit it in half and placed it in the van with the rest of the meat. Bill covered it all with plastic and newspapers. Then he left the disarray of his butchery and picked his way through hooves and guts to the grave site. He lifted the hoe. John came to his side and took the shovel. Gail brushed a strand of hair from her forehead, leaving a bloody streak there. She wiped her hands on her pants and picked up the rake.

The three worked in silence, weaving among the headstones and piles of viscera. An afternoon breeze was coming now, ruffling the hair of the hide and head. They tidied up the grave, smoothed and raked its surface, and then took the flowers from Gail's pile.

The worst ones went first for the bottom, then John tenderly laid the best ones on top. When the last evidence of the beast's intrusion was erased from the grave, John stopped. Gail and Bill handed him their rake and hoe. He turned and walked back to his truck. John put the tools in the bed and climbed into the cab. He started the motor and backed down the drive, away from the two people watching him, and out of sight. — LN

Lee's story presses me with how thoroughly we had lived. My illusion, now gone to fiction? How easily she related to men. Every damn one fell in love with her. But John Tate did lose a son. And in her other story Lee imagined having lost an infant, and I guess she had, the daughter she had not conceived with me. All I could think was that I was not necessary and somehow still liked that state of being. Lee comes less and less to mind, over the years. Though I do remember stuff:

The phone is ringing.

"Tom, it's me. Happy New Year!" Pause. "I just want to know how you are. We're in Paris!"

"Look," I grump, "it's three in the morning . . . sorry . . . just give me a minute. I have to pee."

Lee giggles. "Shit, I thought to call to see . . . I'm sorry. I never even thought about the time difference."

"What's it there? Breakfast?"

"Yes, I just fed the kids and got them to play a game, shut them up for a bit. John is off to a meeting. I'm exhausted already. Never should have brought them. I hear you peeing!"

I put the lid back on the pisspot, an old diaper pail from when the house held many kids.

I can hear Lee's kids gabbling in the background. I remember suddenly how a neighbor lady down the road listened in to our party line calls. We knew because of the canary singing in her kitchen. Lee found that hilarious. I'd invent mildly outrageous things to say that would get around. Not as haplessly as "sperm."

"So, uh, you OK? I'm waking up slowly here."

Lee says, "You've always been slow waking up. Oh…"

"I wouldn't have noticed, eh?" And I do laugh.

She whispers, "I miss you sometimes, when I am not running around."

"Feeling is mutual," I answer.

"Maybe I should never have divorced you. Ha, ha!"

I stop to think. Then say, "Oh yes you should have."

"I love them to death, Tom. I just didn't know how totally consuming they are."

"They'll be in school soon enough, yah?"

"Yes, and John is terrific. He helps as much as he can. I love him. He's thinking of running for the state legislature to try to do something to help with education in the state. Someday I might go back to teaching. He is sort of like Vito…oh…I…"

I interrupt, "You should go back to teaching, you were good at it."

She waits, asks, "Got a squeeze? I assume you are not thinking of marriage."

"No, and I hate the word 'squeeze' or the idea of 'relationship,' like a damaged third party to consider. I have a couple of, what, 'friends.' It's the thing, you know."

"Well, that's good, Tom. You're no absolute loner."

"I am working on poems. And stories. Sort of a fisherman bum now that I have enough to live on. Tired of killing animals. I just mow the gardens, except for salad and Brussels sprouts. Some chard. The easy stuff. Potatoes. I may go to grad school, one of the MFA programs. UVA has already accepted me. Mom's death is still a difficult thing. Her throat kept closing. You remember. You did the Heimlich maneuver for her twice, remember? Anyway, she loved you, said the divorce was my fault. Never trusted me anyway, for not being like Dad. You sound happy."

"Tom, I am. Tom, how is Toby?"

"Pretty somber for a while, but he seems in his usual good spirits. Solid guy. Sam comes around. Toby likes that."

"Hug him for me? I miss him terribly, but he's better off with you and the farm. Toby might have competed with the kids. Keep him with you. For me?"

"Good, I will . . . now can I go back to sleep?"

"You are such a shit!" And she laughs, heartily. "I love you."

"Yep, you too, bye." "Bye." Click.

So I say to Vito, "Don't tell Lee. She said not to push that walk in the woods. I wouldn't listen." "Tom, I cannot tell a lie. I started to tell her that Dell confessed this to me at the bar, but he'd already told John who told Kim who told Lee." At that moment I am standing in the graveyard with a butchered cow in a swarm of blow flies. With cross-hairs on my head. I say so. Vito looks hard at me. "Tom, this is not all about you. Lee worries about you. But let's give this up for now. I must do my ablutions. Is the water in the outside shower still warm?" I tell him it will be a little cool, but probably has some body heat. He rises on his toes, excited. Claps his hands. "I will be right down," and he goes upstairs. I go out on the lawn in the vast moonlight to pee, Toby by my side. Guys don't pee alone, he signals, giving me a glance, goes to the rock wall to cock his leg.

Vito appears in the woodshed door in bright white satin pajamas. He comes out on the lawn, his beautiful head and mane of black hair floating in the overwhelming light that casts the three of our shadows on the grass, Lee's appendages. Toby walks on by and disappears back to bed, to his place. Dogs forgive everything. They have no sense of time, so nothing is ever lost. I am sure he expects her return at any moment. Is somehow content. Vito rolls up his pajama pant legs, turns on the shower spigot and bends, washes his feet in remembrance of Jesus. He does this slowly, with dedication, his feet white ivory. Byzantine. Then Vito rises and looks at me. I step back. "No, Vito, you are not going to wash my feet!" "Are you sure?" he asks. I say, "I'd be a hypocrite." I should apologize and thank him. Or let him wash my feet. But I lack grace. "Well," says Vito, and he laughs, "I mean no *pentola a pressione*, ah, how you say, 'pressure-cooker.' I take seriously that you are not ready to be cleansed, or blessed. You have not committed an interesting sin."

JOE ESUIS

A slightly rolling, gutteral accent. His parents immigrated after WWII, and learned English as needed. His Dad a machinist who repaired older cars in the barn. Townsfolk think Joe sort of oafish. He doesn't sound Downeast, clipped enough, when he does talk. He has driven the schoolbus for seventeen years. He speaks so seldom that kids listen when he does. He hands them down onto ice, positions the bus away from mud in the spring. He redelivers forgotten backpacks or lunch bags to the school cafeteria. He has never had an accident. Joe is big, size fourteen boot, in the same dark blue zippered jumpsuit every day, year in, year out. Buys them at NAPA. Round, bland face and big nose. He has a large plastic thermos to drink coffee from, filled at home from a battered alumi-num percolator . . . out on the dump road in a very neat blue trailer with Betty Penshawe's niece, Clody, not as fat as Betty but getting that way year by year. They have a neutered rescue Rottweiler with a long tail, named Coup.

Joe keeps his Harley Fat Boy under a blue tarp, in the lean-to shed connected to the side of the wooden outhouse. Both of them use the outhouse most of the year, though the trailer has a toilet hooked up to a septic tank. A crosstree spans two yellow birch tree trunks, with a pulley and whiffle-tree for hanging his annual whitetail. He always gets a meat doe, often on opening day of season. Somewhere uphill from his lot. Joe and Clody have TV; a dish hangs on the northeast corner of the trailer's roof. Coup is a love. The breed is known as aloof, but once they sense and like who you are, all pretense is over. He will sit on almost any visitor's feet backwards, as if to look out for, or anchor, keep one from leaving. But few people have experienced Clody's affection. Joe knows everybody. Everybody knows Joe. Hardly anyone talks with him, and never at him. The TV blares all day and flickers evenings.

On an after-school run, delivering kids home, he stops to pick up George "Whack" Ames, who is standing roadside and jerking his hitchhiker's thumb, in his neon orange vest and cap with his father's lever-action Winchester .30-30 held down along his leg. The kids, dozing or looking into their screens in the heat-flooded bus, feel the icy draft when the door jacks open and Whack comes aboard, talking: "Ain't no deer! Too early rut, or somethin'. Seen one small set of tracks, prob'ly yearling. Good thing I picked up that roadkill last month. Had ticks stuffed in 'er nose. Never used to happen. Skinned out

OK. Warden says ticks are bleeding the moose to death, too, 'specially calf. Worse than Massachusetts hunters." He hoots once and starts to light up a cigarette. Joe wags his finger at him. Whack says, "Oops."

The kids up front hear Whack with sleepy indifference. Toward the middle and back, out of earshot, they either doze, stare down into their phone or pad screens, or look without focus out the windows. Leaning mailboxes go by. A downed tree, cut off and cleared at the berm. Mutts come leaping out, barking as the bus passes. Something to do. The kids don't notice that Whack has turned toward them. He rode the bus for years. Whack scans their faces. Says over his shoulder to Joe, "Use' ta be more of us." Headlights from the other direction blaze Whack's cap and vest. Eleven-year-old Suzanne is in the front bench seat. She could reach out and touch the blued steel receiver, hammer and lever. Looks at it idly. There are fewer kids riding the bus now, fewer kids that age in town, some driven to school and picked up by non-working mothers. The girls glance at each other in mutual disdain for the universe, look deeply into their screens.

Whack was not even a fair student, played no sports, never sat in the bleachers but still stands at the end of them, near the end of the players' bench where the cheerleaders sit between cheers. Always red-faced. Like a secret drinker. Slow and quiet observation of Whack by everyone, over many years, has accumulated to no big deal.

Whack was simply passed along through to graduation.

Whack stands there and looks at them, so confident with their electronics and secret language. Whack has never done this, can't type. Joe assumes the rifle is unloaded without thinking about it. Whack is harmless. Few men in town bother to hunt deer anymore. The older ones hate the ATVs roaring around. They don't consider this hunting. They have always hunted on foot, dragged deer on foot back to the road. A few who are overweight or disabled will ride. But most of the deer have moved, not further into the forests, up into the hills, but into the two encroaching housing developments for grass, garden plants, flowering shrubs and shelter in designed patches of decorative paper birch and poplar, as if they know that no hunting is allowed near or among the condos or houses. Or on the new golf course, though that happened one night. Two flashlight poachers with cross-bows from downstate. They got caught. People watch now. They love the deer, regardless of damage. Winters, despite occasional, heavy snows, are warmer, more bare ground than when Whack and Joe were young. The cedar swamps, whitetail winter-feed and "yards" cut down for shingles. Kids no longer "into" hunting. They like soccer, which has replaced football. Cheaper for the school. Joe, being so big and heavy, played center like a wall. When his pickup is running, Whack hangs his Winchester in the back window. He fondles the gun in his sagged recliner in front of the TV. The truck needs a clutch. He is still looking back into the bus at the kids. Some, from the new "village" of duplex condos, will be last to get off, like Suzanne, whose mother walks every day at 4:15 p.m., even in coldest winter dusk, to the gate—for exercise, and to ask her daughter, "How was your day?" Suzanne always works to come up with something to say. Whack remembers the bus as jammed and noisy, some kids sitting on laps of others, or on the aisle floor. Sometimes wrestling. Now the bus is half empty, and quiet. He always tried to stand up with the driver, even when it was Mrs. Jordan, before Joe drove fulltime. Mrs. Jordan was a talker.

Joe pulls over and stops. "Whack, I will let you off now. I am not supposed to do this." Whack turns, shrugs, climbs down and out, not a long walk from the junction and the gravel road where he lives with the uncle and aunt who raised him when his parents divorced, his father career Army, his mother an alcoholic before she died of lung cancer. He didn't make it through Army Basic when he joined up, stands there scanning the windows as the bus slides by and away. Couldn't do the rope climb more than three knots up. Couldn't do more than five chin-ups. Slid back down the slanted wall. Lagged on full pack marches. Some of the kids on that side watch "Whack" disappear, an aspect of the landscape like the dogs, mailboxes, far-apart driveways leading to trailers and old wood houses. Joe sees him fade in the big rear mirror outside the folding door, takes a hard gulp of tepid coffee and speeds up.

NIGHT CLASS

Two days before spring term, the slim, gray, melancholic "18th C Man" is slumped over his desk, a .22 Short in his brain. No one has heard the "crack" so late at night. Though his office door is open. The janitor discovers him at dawn. We chat in front of the maintenance shed where I park my bike. "The Professor" was "a nice man, sorta sad, ya know?" Tenured "men" in the Faculty Lounge say or imply the same . . . how he walked through town with his head down, toting his cracked, duct-taped leather briefcase and his lunch bag, first on the floor in the morning, back after dinner to work late at night when the building is hollow. He apparently had a gentle, cynical wit. My cubicle is next door to his office. I teach at night, but never talked to him. I am not really here, visiting for the year, likely to wind up as a few, perhaps memorable, writerly comments in two or three novice writers' minds. I have assumed that familiar tenured professors, especially in the humanities, where there is no big budget involved, are relatively content and scholarly creatures, some "beloved," and—I tell the janitor—with kids who get free tuition. He offers, "The Professor's are wild; his wife's a townie."

It is not easy to detach from the bloodless image I create in my head, as if he were napping. The stainless steel revolver a paperweight. It may have been blued. His books. His papers half-corrected. I used to fashion myself content. One of the reasons Lee left me. My stoic inertia and penchant for reverie. But that's another story. I have no rights to the Professor's, or to Tim's. But I am a thief.

We are sitting in circled school chairs that hideously screech on the floor. The fire-brick Georgian hall, leprous with ivy, houses this high-ceilinged, dingy yellow room, with municipal fluorescence that casts no shadows of us, where we have come to consider language that might be commensurate with our already fictive lives. I seem to be the only one who thinks so. That our lives become fictions with the passage of each day. We meet Thursday nights for three hours: notably Tim, the Nam vet from southern Indiana, and Henny Ackerman from Holland, research librarian in her early fifties, who has published a story in the *Ohio Review*. Her family's inn alternately filtered Nazi officers and Jewish refugees, the latter helped West in luggers and fishing boats across the Channel. Her new "story" recounts providing food for these various "guests," really an article seeking a story. Probably food as metaphor. Or "serving." Henny says with determination that her parents were atheists, "*a-theist,* not theological." And amateur musicians. She has not fit atheism or music into her piece. She says the Germans pushed her parents to play for them. Piano and cello. What music? I could ask. Does it matter? The Germans demanded what they wanted to eat and drink. Why not music? The refugees ate anything sent from the basement kitchen, up the dumbwaiter to the old servants' garret with the tick mattresses on the floor. "One small chair," Henny says. German leftovers? Chamber pots down and up the same route?

The two chatty young mothers on their night off, one thin, the other ample, also write latent journal entries— one about premarital life, one about life with a child. And about their mothers. I say that journals are OK material. I know they want the entries to be art. But they are getting interested in revision. "Re-seeing," I say. The two under-grad men try adventure stories, sibling rivalry, brothers and friends coming to hate each other briefly—a fistfight over a girl named Viola Thorgersen. And a bicycle. I try to get them to picture what they are writing about and get that into language. What color bicycle? To provide audio. They are picking up on that. I tell them to forget what it means. Let what happens imply that. Another young woman takes poetic interest in a homeless man's attitude toward his dog, a fair correlative for her father's indigence.

This has possibilities if she lets it fly. Why the small class made the course catalog is beyond me, but seven is ideal for a workshop, a luxury really. Each has revised once, to some good effect. Except Tim. All will get As. Why not? "See it all over again, and again," I say. "Let the language as it comes tell you what the story wants to be." I know I can't help anyone "finish" a story. Not like varnishing Plato's table. Good stories, novels, poems finish themselves somewhat incoherently, according to one's lights and emotional involvement. A fitful process. One writes to let the text find the lie that will suffice. Someone said that. I hand them a printout of words by a painter friend in Provincetown:

> Art is reactive. If one peels away motive and influence, what's left is its presence. And that is what is perceived, not the reasons for it being there. I seek evidence for what I make, to make evidence of what I see.

Tonight, Tim Johnson is to read his second draft. He has so far begged off, but tonight he has to do it to be legitimately in the group. To get a grade. He has offered little to the others over the term. His reticence is trusted, just the same. He has let out that he was front line recon, has the shakes—which we can see, like early onset Parkinson's—and is losing tooth after tooth. Blandly handsome, clean-cut, five foot ten or so. Jeans and T-shirt, fatigue jacket over the back of the chair, nondescript but for the shakes and the way he holds his lips pursed, as if to keep his teeth in place. Or is he thinking? He told me in a first-week conference that he is twenty-five years old, that he signed up at eighteen to "do his duty," no idea of Agent Orange, the fog in which he ran zigzag between trenches with his Malinois, Carbo. Carbo is a canine vet now, living with a wheelchair Marine in the boonies near Fayetteville, outside Fort Bragg, amid a loose group of "used-up" vets who Tim says smoke pot and homeschool, shop at the commissary, get checkups at the VA. One of the mothers asks if they are religious. Maybe she homeschools. Tim says, "Not 'specially." He softly reads his plain words. I'll synopsize, with my own visual embellishment. I have to . . . a thief.

Tim and his buddy, D'wan, driving down a jungle road in a jeep camouflaged with mud, hit a Claymore planted by the "Cong," get lifted in the air and tipped over a banking into a concussive nightmare, crashing in suspending undergrowth, a shared dream they wake from under a thatch shed, tied down on their backs, ankles and wrists "secured"—leashed with thongs. Over days they feel no sharp pain and have dulled, achy awareness, but in that waking know what Tim calls "rubbing," and "sort of nice," as small brown girls fondle their genitals like fruit, mount and slide on their erections. Older natives grinning, some toothless, some cackling, some solemn, one with a needle kit from a MASH unit. I see it, but not by Tim's language. Tim and D'wan, drifting on measured heroin. Eyes wandering, they feel whimsical, not tied to their orgasms, alive though badly bruised, scraped and cut. Their waking and sleeping hours a weird reverie. Wet dreams that do not thoroughly wake them. Tim reads on that some kind of leaf, mashed to green paste with piss, gets plastered on their wounds. I relish his few images.

Henny is restless; her hands fidget like chickens, her brown, flounced blouse buttoned up under her chin, a black, open vest, long black skirt and comfortable, clumpy shoes. We are fixed to Tim's voice, so tranquil with authority. Does she, do we, really want Tim's story? As "readers," or writers? Can it grow in us? What does Tim need to do? Do we have to make a movie in our theater-heads of his silhouettes? I, at least, can't help it.

It is Tim's compellingly bland voice that keeps us glued. Is he being honorable? Honoring? Or too off-hand? We strain to hear his intent. Can lack of tone be tone? Tim doesn't seem to think "about" things. Or maybe he does so with such completion that it evokes quiet and a lack of imagery. A warrior's humility? Obviation? There is no useful confusion to resolve. How to afford imagination, to be interior, directing and acting in one's own cinema. Lee felt this as a deflective, often vicarious if not defective facet of my personality.

I wonder how the group responds to Tim's bland,

clinical tone about such bizarre and even comical sex, native fun with the necessary drugs that vets catch hell for. Why did Tim take the workshop? Too many answers for that. Probably "credits." To satisfy the VA?

We respond to Tim, to Tim's voice, period. The oral tradition, strong as any seemingly artless writing. Is Tim's a talent I don't get?

He reads that his buddy D'wan gets free one night and runs across the clearing toward the path down the mountain, so stoned he is sort of dancing, singing, chased by village dogs (as I imagine the scene), so they easily catch up with him: the dogs, and the small, fast, fierce Montagnards, Christian tribal hill people of Nam and Cambodia. Who eat dogs. There are dog meat restaurants in Hanoi. Were they once cannibals? I mean, anyone who would eat a dog...

Lee and I had a fine big Rottweiler named Toby. Tim only mentions Carbo...so lightly. Tim says D'wan is the favored "stud," he "the backup." He smiles a little with this phrase. I wonder if his story could be called "Backup." To get him into it with ironic humor. Catch-22?

So they hack off D'wan's left foot, just above boot top level, with one blow of a heavy machete. Tim hears the heavy blade shatter bone, sees them cauterize the wound with cordite, like an exploding cigar, then stretch red flaps of skin down, fold them, crudely stitch them with dental floss over the charred stump and a wad of the green goo, then *ti* leaves and twine, while D'wan moans, rolls his head and eyes. Tim watches, dazed, from the raised pallet a few feet from D'wan's. Is he still dazed? Tim watches his friend's amputation without need, even now, to believe what he was seeing, saw, is re-seeing. So I direct his scenes in my head. Henny's body sags with pathos, as if she too has taken a hit. It is as if Tim just wants to give us the bones. Make us write it.

Tim ends here, and no one knows anything to say beyond sighs and "Wow, Tim!" He epilogues quite casually that he and D'wan get rescued by a squad of Marines, "choppered in." As if that too were ephemera. I hear the shattering beat of the blades. Are we not to become addicts in Tim's smoky, jungle theater? Our own stories have faded.

Shipped to Tripler, the Kaiser pink hotel on the sunny slopes of O'ahu, Tim and D'wan do rehab: "We were 'all done,' they told us." Months of walking in long hallways with nurses and trainers, working out in a gym and heated pool. Months indoors, with "outings" to *heiaus*, the Waikiki Aquarium, charitable restaurants like Zippy's where clientele applaud them; sports bars for football, baseball or the NBA; Buddhist temples, the outlook at the Pali, a busload of wounded vets to see where Kamehameha forced a thousand Marquesans off the cliff with a cannon supplied by a British merchant vessel. Lee and I knew these details from a long visit to O'ahu.

Tim called it all "rehab," period. What he wrote did not include D'wan, with a prosthetic foot, shooting baskets. Henny tells him to write that. The athletic young man in the class wonders out loud about runners' "blades," their springiness, and how someone like D'wan might "dunk" if he wore one, D'wan's rehab being well before "Cheetah" technology. Can one wear just one blade and stay balanced? The class deflects from Tim's reticence. Tim says he was kept in the hospital to help D'wan get on with his life, though he, too, had continual counseling and observation . . . for his "shakes." Did staff notice something about Tim besides the "shakes" and loose teeth? Symptoms they could not attribute to Agent Orange for fear of political repercussions? Did, does, Tim seem self-destructive in his apparent impassivity? Or is he always existentially placid? PTSD doesn't exist as a subject yet. In WWI and II they referred to "shell shock." A phrase less euphemistic than Post-Traumatic Stress Disorder. Did Tim's experience generate the syndrome? Is he curious enough? Was he ever?

Henny breaks silence, asks Tim, "How are you doing?" Tim says his teeth will have to go for dentures, but the shakes will take time, if ever. Then Tim grins, his lips together, softly says, "I have no time." Henny asks, "What?" Tim says, "Time's a joke." Tim is commenting on something? "No time to go to work. No job. No time for my daughter, except for homework. Smarter than I am, busy with friends, school, my aunt. No time for TV, even baseball, because I don't care. No time for being 'down,' no time for food, no time for joking around, no time for women. No time for buddies' services, too many offing themselves, one way or the other. A dozen a day, maybe more. No time for remembering the 'Monkey Faces'…spotted, ranged, targeted. No time for anger. No fucking time…sorry for cursing."

Where did this come from? Shouldn't he write it? How to intrude? Tim has just exploded, serenely.

Henny objects, but not to Tim's cuss word. Says her family saved Jews and that names like "Monkey Face" are Nazi. Tim leans a little forward, says, "Ma'am, I married one."

He says that he married a Saigon local and brought her and her two boys "stateside." That she is an ARVN officer's widow. So exotic, I imagine, that he mistook her intentions for love. Have I become a cynic about marriage? He lives with the daughter they have between them, with his aunt tonight. Tim lazily fills the silence. "I'm on relief, go to the VA for drug tests to keep my support check— they put up with a little pot. That pays us to live with my parents, basically broke, using their car. It's OK. Don't want to sell the old place. Land went years ago. Couldn't make enough to live anywhere else. A close thing."

Tim pauses, then continues. "She watched TV in the

bedroom to learn English. Damn well. Didn't like my parents pushing for her to go to church with them. Buddhist. They walked down the drive every day to wait for the school bus to take and return the boys. She did do some housework, always sweeping. Dishes. Kind with our baby." Tim pauses, as if to consider whether to add, "Wore high heels or went barefoot in the house all the time. Ran away with the State Farm insurance guy who came to sell us a policy. Took her two. Happens to other guys." Then, "Whittled her chopsticks from twigs in the yard."

I am almost howling, "So write it!"

Henny tears up. The rest look down, have nothing to say. What I might say is, "Tim, this isn't a story to be picked at . . . yet. The part about the Montagnards and being captured might be seen through the heroin, the dreams, the girls, the forest, the Montagnards in their environment." My corny impulses. Publication and sales? A movie? The jeep wreck. I think of his wife's cocoa feet. We saw plenty of that beauty in Hawaii, when Lee took a half year off and her parents paid for us to "go relax." Which meant, "Get pregnant." Hawaiian light in mixed Asian/Polynesian skin is a miracle. Mainlanders don't think of Hawaii as an Asian culture. It is now: Filipino, Japanese, Chinese, "poi" (some haole and some pure Polynesian), Hawaiian, Samoan, Tongan. Refugees from the Marshalls. Anyway, I say, "Make a movie with words. Check out *Apocalypse Now* and *The Deer Hunter,* because the story you want us to feel isn't in your facts, but in how you use words to make us feel it, right down to the color of the State Farm necktie. In other words, play God with it, if you have to." Is this teaching? Could I use the term "objective correlative" in Tim's world? His nameless "I." Or Henny's?

Tim says *The Deer Hunter* "gets it."

Maybe the war really does make Tim not give a shit. Residue heroin aura, tapered with pot? I want desperately to tinker with Tim's "facts," just as I make fictions of my own "real" life. Movies of pasts. Accuracy not important. Why quote Barry Lopez, who said that we write stories to keep each other from being afraid? Tim? Helping us? And of what am I afraid? Does Tim give a shit about empathy?

Did I really say, "If you want to, need to, the story can expand about your wife. Did she try to escape the war, too? By getting away from you? With State Farm? No joke, did she think that was Communism? Had she been a Cong sympathizer? Did you escape? What is insurance? What color were those heels? Maybe write it to D'wan? Or for him. You have the seeds of a novel about war and race and culture, especially American. And you do have time . . . time, and maybe dreams. God help that State Farm guy."

Tim smiles, so everyone does.

I think of how hard it is for me to talk or write about Lee. She thought I could be a family man, that I wouldn't be apathetic about that. I like to think that "family" just didn't happen, and that's that. But I was relieved. I can agree with Vito…no interesting sin here. Beyond doubts about the future of humanity. Kent State put a dent in any optimism.

"Seriously, it can be a terrific story," I blather on. "Do you know what happened to your wife? How did the Montagnard village smell? Could you just reimagine it for us? And D'wan's life?"

Tim says, "His leg smelled like chicken frying."

Silence. I feel like a damn fool, remember the dog carrying a human hand in *Yojimbo*. I know then that Tim can write. Henny takes us back: "But why would they tie you down? Cut off D'wan's foot?"

Tim says, "Oh, hill girls with half white or black kids, *bui doi,* get full commissary privileges. Feed the village. Fifty thousand of them with American blood left behind. Hated. I took our kid and hers home with me. Didn't work out, that's all. Some *bui doi* in Fayetteville. My daughter is *bui doi,* but she don't know it yet. Nga's boys pure Vietnamese. She already had a commissary pass." "Nga" means "beautiful girl." *Bui doi* means "dust of life."

I remember the night of November 3, 1962, on our second "honeymoon" on O'ahu.

For three nights we had driven up the snake road onto Tantalus to the overlook, to see the Johnson Island hydrogen bomb explode. Each night it was postponed for atmospheric reasons. We almost gave up the fourth night, but went anyway, sat on the fenders looking down and out across the Pacific to the south. At 11:53 p.m. the horizon silently lit up; pale, ghoulish green light spread toward us like a tidal wave, X-rayed Honolulu's down-town, Waikiki, Diamond Head, Ewa to the west. Then the light spread upwards and turned magenta in the upper atmosphere, as if to rain down on us like fingers of blood. The birds began to sing, thinking it was dawn. We wept.

I still "see" the 10.4 megaton blast, two hundred and fifty miles high, July 16, 1962, eight hundred miles south of O'ahu, at 11:38 p.m. The X-ray and bloody runnels. I hear the doves, mynahs and cardinals singing for dawn. I still see Terry Luke, two cars down, take photos of that sky while Patricia Lei Anderson, just crowned Miss Hawaii in the Waikiki Shell for being lovely, sings "Un bel dì" in full *holoku,* see in that sky her glory and evening's end.

I use this event to convince myself that it is OK to not want children. Lee would have thought it a cheap shot if I told her.

I walk out of class, having thanked Tim for so much to think about, saying that we'll just talk and ask questions during the last class, meet at O'Hara's, have a beer. My bike is parked in the dark across the green by the janitor's metal shed. I put my class register and copies to put final comments on in the saddle bags and settle the helmet on my head. I use the electric starter instead of the kick start and "she" purrs into being, the horizontal twin pistons slapping nicely in the cylinders. A BMW R69S already a decade old, quiet and dependable. Black, with white pinstripes on the fenders. Europe's police bike. Once I thought of telling Henny, who had said to "be careful" when she saw that helmet in class, that a Jewish pal—seeing my BMW designed for Rommel—said they were made quiet for sneaking up on Jews. I took this as a joke at the time. The internal drive shaft kept out Saharan sand that would destroy conventional drive chains. I turn on the original six-volt jaundiced headlight and head off along the tarmac path, empty now of students. Henny walked out with Tim.

I turn off the boulevard and onto the twisty two-lane that the Beemer loves, heading toward the hamlet southwest where I rent a small farmhouse away from the campus on its classic hill. Driving a motorcycle means no dreaming or letting other stuff bother. Out of my mind I go along, at one with the bike, and pass the old coal miner's bar, the Rainbow, sunken below road level and famous for its six pool tables. I play there with the "Chaucer Man," Roy—ex-Marine, Korea, light heavyweight boxing champ of the Pacific theater, who fought in a ring set up on a carrier deck. GI Bill PhD. A pickup swings up onto the road behind me and I see it come closer and closer in my mirrors. No going faster on the winding road. My body tightens, he is that close to my ass end, his headlights weaving. I try to stay far right on a few short straightaways, hoping he will pass, but he looms over my back like something deserved. We start down the long hill to the intersection. I can't slow down and don't dare speed up, praying I get to the well-lit gas station and pull off. I finally do and the son of a bitch pulls right in, goes around me to a bay and gets out, starts unloading a tire. Lanky, gaunt bastard, sad red flannel shirt, John Deere tractor cap. I lift off my helmet and re-cinch the straps, so I can swing it like a pail of rocks. I walk to him, saying, "You could have killed me." He looks up, narrowly, and sort of whispers, "Ah, boosheet." He is so drunk I quit, and as I turn back by his pickup I see the two babies, maybe three or four years old, standing on the front seat with their palms on the dash. Their faces are tired. One gapes. I don't want kids.

I go back to my bike. Thinking about Lee, how she complained: "I can't see around you or over you! It's damned boring." Yet I have kept my bike. Lost her. I am already thinking about the bike, though: "Time to give up this romance." Or will that go on? Is Tim a solo now, too, or has he always been one? Have I? No, he obviously loves his daughter. I swing my leg over the seat, boot down on the peg. I press the starter button, hear the engine begin again with a soft cough, the oil-rich horizontal pistons happy, happy. Everything, it's all here. Tim, Henny, Lee. The drunk. The babies. The danger. I think: "I would prefer not to." Yet I love life at the same time. Someone or no one is always right behind me, in my fictitious life. I can't slow down and I can't speed up. There really are cross-hairs on my head. I am pretty sure Tim, in my place, would toss it off.

I have already packed my box of books for mailing on to Provincetown for the summer. No next gig, yet. I am bored with the collection of stories, ending with a novella, that I am revising for an indie press. Set in a very rural, coastal Maine community that I lived pretty thoroughly in, once. Lee remarried to a school administrator, has two kids. She called one New Year's Eve from Paris, where they'd gone with the kids, who she said were driving her nuts. And, lightly, "Maybe I shouldn't have left you." "Yes, you should have," I answered. "You shithead," she laughed. Alone, I hadn't taught yet, hadn't published anything to get me work. I wasn't worried. What has my temperament saved me for?

I have to sell the bike. It is too collectible. Too many guys stop to look at it. I "know" a van with an acetylene torch will come, cut the chain lock and steal the bike. And the drunk in the pickup has frightened me. Besides, it is the perfect bike. Can't handle that.

Department hallways are eerily quiet at night, except for the humming of the buffer machine that endlessly polishes the floors. All over the country. I drop my grades into the slot in the English department office door. I hear again the "crack" of the pistol that I never heard.

In P-town, after a long, cool ride on 90 by Cleveland, Buffalo, Albany and Stockbridge, four nights in cheap motels, I settle into my efficiency in a house behind Napi's, start looking over my latest drafts. They always seem as though someone else wrote them. I finally track Tim through the West Roxbury VA hospital, write a note to encourage him to make "the" book. Ask if he's OK. "How's D'wan?" I want to be rid of this story. Give it back. Or do I? I did nothing for him. Tim writes back. Typing, I am sure, slowly. He'd said in workshop that his handwriting was getting too shaky. I have a pal who died of Parkinson's recently. Much older than Tim.

Hey, thanks. We got cots in a buddy's garage near Orlando. Too hard on the kid in Indiana. Eat off a card table. The kid watches cartoons. Does her homework. I watch a little baseball. Fishing shows. Cartoons. Half-assed. Set on 24/7. She likes that too. Shakes are bad, no real sleep except naps before she comes home on the bus. No VA drugs. Don't trust them. Pot. My Dad had a stroke, watches squirrels off the porch. Or the Weather Channel with the volume off. Oh yeah,

D'wan offed himself in a TR3, drunk or iced on Tantalus. Took a hapa girl with him. Weekends I do some football. Don't care who wins, beers with deep fried triple-tail at Durfy's on Friday . . . couple other vets come pick me up. Three times a week, four wall handball at Central Y. Only time the shakes don't queer me. New teeth. I like triple tail. Other fish hard to taste. Thinking what you said. Some words here and there. No PC. Too fast for me. My little girl gettin' by. Black kids in her school, and Mex. Loves music and art. Going to be a beauty. Maybe a book or something someday. Go easy. Thanks again, Tim.

ps. thought you'd get a kick out of me playing hand-ball. Know you play. Started with rehab sport classes in Orlando. Not very good at it, play with a priest. He's real good, great hands, mean mouth. Disses me all the time. "Wimp!" Leave my teeth in the locker. Game beats pot. Don't really play Father John. Just the ball.

ACKNOWLEDGMENTS

Certain stories in this volume have appeared in the following publications: "Dog Watch" in *The Green Mountain Review*; "Refrigerator Church" in *The Long Story*; "Just for Eggs" in *The Long Story*; "#2 Iron" in *drafthorse*; and "Night Class" in *The Deadly Writers Patrol*.

Certain poems in the story "Gloria Artichokes" have appeared in the following publications: "Turtle" in *Constellations*; "Milking" in *Ploughshares*; "Delivery" in *Natural Bridge*; and "Nana's Lime Green Easy" in *Avatar*.

ABOUT THE AUTHOR

PAUL NELSON was born near Boston of Norwegian and Finnish immigrants and was raised mostly in Maine. He attended Dartmouth College on an athletic scholarship and was an officer in the U.S. Navy for three years. After graduate work at Colgate University, he taught high school in Hawaii, and was a college teacher in Vermont, Indiana, and Colorado before becoming a Professor of English and Director of Creative Writing for Ohio University. He has published nine books of poetry, including the critically acclaimed *Days Off* (University Press of Virginia, 1982 AWP Winner). He and his wife, the painter Judith Nelson, currently live, write and paint on the Olympic Peninsula, near the necessary ocean and in the northern light of their forebears.